"I'll do whate

Gus smiled weakly
for you."

Mia looked away, f

He winced as he shifted in his chair.

"You need to lie down." She stood and started clearing the table. "When did you take your last dose of medication?"

"I'm supposed to wait another hour," he grunted.

"I've got to get going. I need to get over to the clinic. Will you be okay by yourself for a little while?"

"Yep."

"I'll help you get back to the couch." She put the dishes and cups in the sink, then morphed into caretaker mode.

It was easier that way. Then she didn't have to think about how Gus and Abner had been closer than brothers. Or how these complicated feelings for her late fiancé's best friend were clouding her judgment. Falling for Gus was *not* an option.

Because if she wasn't careful, those piercing blue eyes and his calming presence would just keep reeling her in. And she wouldn't allow herself to love another man who might surrender his life to the sea…

Heidi McCahan is a Pacific Northwest girl at heart, but now resides in North Carolina with her husband and three boys. When she isn't writing inspirational romance novels, Heidi can usually be found reading a book, enjoying a cup of coffee and avoiding the laundry pile. She's also a huge fan of dark chocolate and her adorable goldendoodle, Finn. She enjoys connecting with readers, so please visit her website, heidimccahan.com.

Books by Heidi McCahan

Love Inspired

Home to Hearts Bay

An Alaskan Secret
The Twins' Alaskan Adventure
His Alaskan Redemption

The Firefighter's Twins
Their Baby Blessing
An Unexpected Arrangement
The Bull Rider's Fresh Start

Visit the Author Profile page at LoveInspired.com.

His Alaskan Redemption

Heidi McCahan

LOVE INSPIRED
INSPIRATIONAL ROMANCE

LOVE INSPIRED®

INSPIRATIONAL ROMANCE

ISBN-13: 978-1-335-58635-3

His Alaskan Redemption

Love Inspired
22 Adelaide St. West, 41st Floor
Toronto, Ontario M5H 4E3, Canada
www.LoveInspired.com

Printed in U.S.A.

When thou passest through the waters,
I will be with thee; and through the rivers,
they shall not overflow thee: when thou walkest
through the fire, thou shalt not be burned;
neither shall the flame kindle upon thee.
—*Isaiah* 43:2

For my sweet friend Anna—you are one of the best people I know. Thank you for encouraging me and cheering me on as I chase a big dream.

Chapter One

Mia Madden rarely second-guessed her decisions.

Raised on an island in the middle of an unforgiving ocean, she'd learned to adapt to severe weather, grounded flights, even delayed package deliveries. Living in Hearts Bay, Alaska, often required embracing a Plan B. Despite the obstacles and harsh elements of island living, she thrived in her role as a physician assistant. Nothing brought her more satisfaction than responding to illnesses, acute injuries and even life-threatening emergencies.

Until tonight.

Tonight, she wished she'd silenced her phone. Or left the thing charging on the kitchen counter, instead of falling asleep with it lying on the mattress beside her. She blamed the late-night internet sleuthing. Ever since her mother's health had rapidly declined last summer, Mia had embarked on a desperate quest to find a viable treatment. The specialist they'd visited in Seattle had recommended a bone-marrow transplant as the best option to combat the aplastic anemia.

Mom had insisted they take a break from searching for a donor and focus on the holidays, but Mia hadn't backed off. They didn't have the luxury of slowing down. How was she supposed to sit back and do nothing when Mom was battling fatigue and frequent infections? Mia had done enough research to know that if the condition wasn't treated effectively, heart failure was a real possibility.

And they couldn't lose Mom. Her family had suffered enough loss already.

Finding a donor wasn't the only challenge keeping Mia awake at night. Someone she'd never met, Lexi Thomas, had contacted her three weeks ago and insisted they'd been switched at birth. How was it possible? Did her parents know? She hadn't worked up the courage to ask them. The notion that she might have a different family in a small town in Georgia wasn't something she wanted to think about. It was too shocking. The kind of thing that only happened in a book or a movie. She couldn't ignore Lexi forever, though. Other than acknowledging she'd received the message and needed time to process, Mia hadn't initiated a follow-up conversation. The woman deserved an answer, and Mia felt a little sick admitting it, but they might need Lexi in the very near future.

That was a dilemma to resolve another day. Tonight, her patients deserved her full attention.

She trudged across the hospital's dark parking lot, one gloved hand clutching the hood of her parka over her head as she hunched her shoulders against the blowing snow. When she'd answered Dr. Rasmussen's midnight call a few minutes ago, the tremor in his voice had sent an uneasy feeling skittering down her spine. The man was a legend. Hearts Bay's beloved physician of over thirty years. If he was overwhelmed, how in the world would she handle whatever waited inside the emergency room?

Floodlights beside the building illuminated the bright orange Coast Guard Jayhawk sitting on the helipad, its rotors spinning. She averted her gaze then quickened her pace, determined not to let the sight of that stupid helicopter undo her. Almost four years had passed since her brother, Charlie, and her fiancé, Abner Rossi, passed away in a boating accident. She still couldn't look at the rescue helicopter without thinking of that horrible day.

Don't. Not now.

Revisiting those painful memories would only send her mentally to a place she couldn't afford to go. Before she could swipe her employee badge, the automatic doors opened with a whoosh. Dr. Rasmussen stepped outside. The rumble of the ambulance's diesel engine punctured the night air as the vehicle backed into the bay.

"Thanks for coming in, Mia," Dr. Rasmussen said. "This is our seventh victim right here."

"Motor-vehicle accident?" She glanced toward the driver as he and his partner jumped from the cab and jogged around toward the back doors of the ambulance.

"Fishing vessel. Seven crab fishermen went overboard. The storm is brutal. Everyone made it off the boat alive, thanks to the Coast Guard's quick maneuvers and their rescue swimmers, but I really need you to bring your A game tonight."

"Of course," she said, even though the cautious side of her brain sounded the evasive-maneuver alarm and her limbs tingled with the urge to flee.

"I'll see you inside." He turned to speak to the EMTs.

Mia swiped her badge then hurried into the ER. The warm air and familiar antiseptic smell greeted her. They'd been woefully understaffed this week after a nasty stomach virus had kept more than half their employees at home.

"Hey, Mia. The guy behind curtain number three is all yours." Tammy Adams, a seasoned nurse and the mother-in-law of Mia's sister Eliana, wheeled the crash cart down the corridor. "We're swamped."

"Got it." She barely squeezed out the words. She shed her jacket and dropped it on a chair in the nurses' station. The tightness in her chest scared her. Usually, a situation like this was right in her wheelhouse. But any kind of accident related to the water still provoked fear. Undermined her confidence. Okay, so seven victims might overwhelm their depleted staff, especially in the middle of a January storm, but she could still do her part.

Right?

She looped a stethoscope around her neck, jammed her phone in the pocket of her scrubs, then strode toward the makeshift cubicles designated for triage patients. The doors behind her slid open again and cold air swept in, swirling around her legs. The EMTs rushed in, transporting the man on the stretcher into the corridor. Dr. Rasmussen trailed behind, calling out instructions.

Mia slid a disposable mask in place, then squirted a generous dollop of hand sanitizer into her clammy hands and rubbed her palms together. Drawing a deep breath, she pushed aside the curtain. An orange survival suit and heavy-duty brown rubber boots had been discarded on the gray speckled linoleum and the sight made her legs quake.

The man reclining on the bed groaned. One large hand braced his other arm across his broad chest. Slowly, he turned his head toward the curtained entrance. His handsome features crimped.

Those familiar icy blue eyes bore into her. "Mia?"

His voice made her heart pinch. Her patient was an injured crabber. And not just any crab fisherman, either. The shock of white-blond hair and ruddy splotches of color that clung to his strong cheekbones were impossible to forget. Gustav Coleman, her late fiancé's best friend, had survived yet another accident.

"Wh-what are you doing here, Gus?"

Stupid, stupid question. She was supposed to ask him to rate his pain on a scale of one to ten. Or wiggle his fingers. She should check his pupils' reaction to light in case he had a concussion. There were so many crucial pieces of information she needed to gather in order to assess his condition. Instead, demanding to know why he was in *her* hospital seemed critical to her mission. Because everything about this awful scenario felt terribly familiar.

Her brother and fiancé had met their watery demise in a capsized fishing vessel. It was an accident Gus had avoided because he'd been a no-show and the boat had left port without him. Yeah, she was probably supposed to forgive him for surviving, but she couldn't.

The guy behind curtain number three is all yours. Tammy's directive reminded her that she had a job to do. Even if she wanted nothing to do with him.

Gus tried to shift onto his side, but grimaced. His skin was turning a terrifying shade of pale blue. She stuck her head back out the curtain. "I need help in here."

"My chest." He squinted up at her and clawed at his grimy plaid button-down. "Hurts."

His pain propelled her into action. She moved to his side, and with trembling fingers, searched for his pulse first at his wrist and then at his neck. "Can you tell me anything about what happened, Gus?"

"My body hit…the railing. Went overboard… Really hurts…" His gravelly voice trailed off as he struggled to breathe.

Blunt trauma to the chest. Struggling to breathe. Rapid, weak pulse. She mentally catalogued his symptoms. "Do you have pain on the left side or the right side of your chest?"

"I don't… I don't know. It all hurts," he mumbled. Then his eyelids fluttered shut.

She quickly unbuttoned his plaid flannel shirt. "I'm going to help you."

A nurse joined her. "What can I do?"

"I'm concerned about a possible rib fracture that may have punctured his lung. We've got to work quickly. This could be a traumatic pneumothorax."

The nurse handed her a pair of shears. Mia slit his white T-shirt in half and pushed it aside. Her breath caught at the sight of the gray-blue ink on his chest. The letters *CM* and *AR*. Gus had Charlie and Abner's initials tattooed on his skin? Her legs wobbled and she clutched the bed railing.

The nurse studied her. "Mia. Are you okay?"

"Yeah." She closed her eyes for a second. "I, um… Gus and I go way back, that's all."

She flung a silent prayer for strength toward heaven, then opened her eyes. Gus writhed in agony on the gurney. He was supposed to have been the best man at her wedding. A wedding that had never happened because Abner and her brother had been taken far too soon.

None of that mattered when there were lives at stake. *Come on. Focus.*

"Stay with me, Gus. I'm going to get you through this. I promise."

She pushed aside the painful memories that threatened to steal her concentration and helped the nurse prep Gus for a procedure to reinflate his lung. She'd do her best to save his life. Even if he was the last person she ever wanted to see again.

Broken bones and a capsized boat weren't part of his plan.

Gus squinted against the morning light glowing behind the window blinds, then slammed his eyes shut. He wasn't ready to face the day. Between the pain in his chest and arm, frequent interruptions from the nurse to check on him and activity outside his room, he'd slept in short, fitful bursts.

At least he had survived.

He wanted to be grateful. Scratch that. He *was* grateful. It was just that the timing really stank. Finally, after years of struggling, he'd made peace with his past. Crabbing was all he knew, all he wanted to do, and he'd found a position on a boat with a great crew. Ironically, with a captain who had a stellar reputation for running a safe operation. This was going to be his season. No more excuses. He'd ditched the victim mentality and welcomed the New Year with a promise that he'd be the man his little girl needed him to be.

But how could he provide for a child when he'd lost his livelihood and the use of his arm? A tremor wracked his battered body as he mentally replayed the nightmare that had unfolded only hours ago. Ice had solidified on every surface. Waves washed over the bow, and the winds howled, dousing the crew in freezing spray. They'd swung baseball bats and hammers, and even heaved a few rubber mallets— any tool they could find—to break up the ice and keep the boat from listing under the weight. His crewmates' screams as they slid off the deck and plunged into the bone-chilling Gulf of Alaska had been an awful sound he'd never forget.

Gus shifted in the bed, desperate for a more comfortable position. The sling helped stabilize his shoulder and broken collarbone, but even the slightest movement made him grit his teeth against the pain. The three cracked ribs weren't helping, either. He had outsmarted death, but his injuries rendered him useless. No captain would take a one-armed deckhand. He had to get back out there, though. Too much was at stake. With only six weeks left in crabbing season, he desperately needed at least one more good run.

Especially since everything they'd caught yesterday had gone down with the boat.

The realization filled his stomach with a hollow ache. He wasn't supposed to focus on the lost income, considering some of his crew-mates might've lost their lives. The boat's crew and their families waiting back in Dillingham would never be the same if their men didn't come home.

Hinges on the door squealed and light spilled in from the corridor, silhouetting a woman as she stepped inside the room pushing a cart.

"Mr. Coleman, good morning," she greeted him. "We brought you breakfast."

"Gus?" It was a different voice. One that he knew from memory.

"Mia?" He could barely get her name past his parched throat.

She paused next to his bed and reached for a switch. The fluorescent light mounted on the wall overhead flickered on. "How are you feeling?"

Grunting, he squinted against the light. His mouth felt like he'd swallowed a bag of cotton balls. "I've had better days."

"Same." Her flawless features stretched into a weary smile. Her hopeful expression and polite smile buoyed him, helped him push through the pain and the medication fog. He surveyed her creamy skin and auburn hair, which was twisted into a bun. Basked in the concern filling her green eyes. Behind her, the woman pushed the cart closer. The aroma of scrambled eggs and oatmeal made him queasy.

"Thanks, Beth. I'll take it from here," Mia said.

"You're welcome. Have a good day, sir." The woman offered a polite nod then left the room.

Mia pulled a penlight from the pocket of her scrubs. "On a scale of one to ten, how's your pain?"

He didn't want to admit it, but everything hurt. He had to get out of here, though. Had to get back on another boat. More importantly, he had to get back to Dillingham so he could take care of his little girl. Poppy wasn't quite two yet, and his ex-wife was quite controlling when it came to making childcare arrangements. She'd give him a hard time if he didn't show up for his weekend visit with their daughter.

"Gus, can you rate your pain for me?" Mia lifted her stethoscope from around her neck. "Scale of one to ten."

"Six, or maybe a seven." He clenched his teeth against a white-hot sensation stabbing him under his shoulder blade.

"We're going to try and get some food in you,

and it will be time for more meds soon. It's best if we try and stay ahead of that pain."

Too late. He fumbled under the sheet for the button that raised his bed.

"What do you need?" she asked.

"I need to get out of here."

Worry creased her brow. "Not yet. I need to reassess your injuries. You might have to stay at least one more day."

"No, you don't understand." He jabbed at the remote control beside him. Nothing happened.

"Here. You need to be careful. Let's try sitting up." She took the plastic device from his hand and the bed elevated slowly. He swallowed back a growl. Just that subtle movement made him miserable.

"You have several fractured ribs. We put your shoulder back in its socket and you've had a tension pneumothorax."

"What's that?"

"Your lung collapsed, pushing air out into your chest. It's a life-threatening situation, mainly because it compromises your cardiac function, as well as your ability to breathe."

"Wow, Doc, you got any good news?"

Her lips tipped up in a half smile. "I'm a physician assistant, not a doctor. The good news is we saved your life."

"Great. Thanks." Stabbing pain returned to

his chest. He tried to staunch the sensation by pressing his hand to his side. It didn't help.

"I'd like to check your vitals again. Were you able to sleep at all?"

"Not really." He tried to breathe normally but the warmth of her hand brushing against his skin as she dipped her stethoscope inside his gown had him distracted.

Easy, tiger. This is Abner's girl.

"We need to talk about next steps. In your current condition, you can't fly on an airplane for at least two weeks. You're going to need to learn to manage that chest tube and I'll refer you to physical therapy. Do you have any family in Hearts Bay?"

Chest tube? He glanced down. Sure enough, a shoelace-like tube protruded from under his gown and snaked into a container somewhere beside his bed. "How long do I have to have that?"

"A few days." She removed the stethoscope. "Once we're confident your lung has reinflated properly and there's no infection, we'll remove it. You didn't answer. Any family close by?"

"No. My brother lives in Montana, my mom's in New Mexico looking after my grandfather and my sister and daughter are in Dillingham."

Her eyes widened, then she looked away.

Did the news that he was a father bother her?

They hadn't exactly kept in touch after Abner's memorial service. He'd lived a lot of life in the last four years. Maybe she had, too. He stole a glance at her left hand. No ring. Interesting.

"Let me evaluate your pupils." She leaned closer and he couldn't help but notice a strand of hair had slipped loose and framed her heart-shaped face. "How old is your little girl?"

"Poppy. She's almost two. And, man, what a firecracker." Thinking about his daughter soft-ened the edges of the pain digging into him. "She's the reason I have to get back to fishing. Crab season will be over in several weeks. I can't afford not to be out there right now."

She straightened and put the penlight back in her pocket. Her pretty eyes filled with em-pathy. "Gus, I get it. You want and need to be fishing, but your vessel sank. Your injuries are significant." She frowned. "No captain in his right mind should have you on his crew in your condition. It would be dangerous, possi-bly even life-threatening, if you went back out there now."

He fisted the covers in his uninjured hand. Frustration swelled in his gut. Her prognosis wasn't something he could accept. There was too much at stake. Besides, plenty of men fished with injuries. That was life at sea. Crabbers had the most dangerous job in the world.

"Let's try eating and drinking for now. How about some water?" She offered a plastic cup with a lid and a straw.

"I got it." He took it from her. There was no way he was going to let her feed him like he was an infant.

"Little sips," she prompted quietly.

He took a drink. The cold water hit the back of his throat and shocked him. He swallowed, determined not to cough because he knew from past experience that coughing with fractured ribs burned like fire.

Mia's scrubs brushed together as she turned toward the cart and slid it closer. He shifted his gaze to the food sitting on the tray. Arguing with her wouldn't get him anywhere, but there was no way he could handle scrambled eggs yet.

"I have an idea." She faced him again. "My parents have a guesthouse on their property. It's supposed to be for my grandmother, but she won't move into town."

He did not like where this was going.

She shrugged and blew out a breath. "That's a long story. Anyway, it's vacant right now. I'm sure my folks wouldn't mind having you stay there. You can—"

"No, I can't. I've got to get back to Dillingham."

"That's not possible. Last time I checked,

there are no roads to Dillingham, so you'd have to fly. Or take a very long, painful boat ride. I can't let you get on a plane. The change in pressure might cause your lung to collapse again."

"You don't understand. Poppy's mom is a police officer. She's very driven and insists that we split childcare evenly. I can't—" A sharp wave of pain crested. He clamped his mouth shut to keep from groaning.

"Could your sister watch your daughter?"

"How long?"

"You have to wait fourteen days to fly, and more than likely it will be six weeks until you're able to work."

"You've got to be kidding. There's no way. I've got to find a position on another crab boat as soon as possible."

"Like I said, no captain should let a man in your condition on his boat."

"But I can't afford to be out that long." Gus fought to keep the panic from seeping into his voice.

If he didn't work, how could he give Poppy the stability she needed? Sure, his sister had offered to take care of his daughter if he got in a pinch, but she already had a family of her own.

"I'm sorry I don't have better news."

Gus tamped down a terse response. This had to be hard for her. Probably brought back memories of what happened with her brother and Abner.

"Other than your boots and your clothes, we haven't located any of your personal items. If you need to call someone, I'm happy to help you get in touch with a family member or a friend."

Despair blanketed him. The reality that his wallet, photographs and expensive gear were probably somewhere on the ocean floor made him want to cuss. He didn't talk like that anymore. But sometimes in his weaker moments, he struggled.

"Maybe you could call your sister or your mom this afternoon and let them know what happened. Think about my offer. I won't discharge you until we know you have a safe place to go and access to physical therapy."

Gus looked away and scoffed. "Great. Thanks."

"Take care, Gus." She moved toward the door. "I'm glad you fared better than most of your crewmates."

By the time Gus processed her comment, the door had swung closed. *Most* of his crewmates? What did that mean? He fumbled under the blanket for that buzzer thingy to call for someone to answer his questions, then changed his mind. Mia's vague update was probably all he was going to get. If he pressed for more details, she'd remind him there were rules about privacy and sharing patients' information. Evidently a near-drowning experience still didn't earn him the right to know how his buddies were doing.

Guilt, his long-lost nemesis, slipped in. What if he was the only survivor? That couldn't be. Mia would've told him.

Wouldn't she?

He'd spent years feeling guilty about the horrid abuse he'd avoided because his brother and sister had suffered to protect him. Abner and Charlie's deaths only compounded the guilt. Gus closed his eyes and rubbed his fingers over the gown covering his tattoo. He should've been on board Charlie Madden's boat that day. Except he'd drank too much the night before and gone home with a woman whose name he couldn't recall. He'd overslept. The boat had left him behind, and Charlie and Abner never came home.

He couldn't blame Mia if she still held it against him.

After his brief marriage to Liesel had fallen apart last year, he'd become a Christian. His counselor provided plenty of coping strategies to process the layers of guilt and regret that had almost buried him. If not for his baby girl and his newfound faith, he might've given up.

Because forgiving himself had proven to be the hardest step of all.

"Lord, I'm new at this prayer thing," he

whispered. "Please help me. I need to get well quickly, so I can make a living, and be the dad my daughter needs."

A ball of emotion filled his throat. He couldn't finish the prayer. It hurt too much to admit, even to God, that he'd failed the people he loved the most. Again.

She couldn't *not* help him.

The thought kept rolling around in her weary mind. Mia blinked against the grit in her eyes and peered at the computer screen. Only one more electronic chart to update, then she could go home. Except she couldn't stop thinking about Gus. Since she'd left his bedside a few minutes ago, her heart had battled her brain. He needed a place to stay and assistance with everyday activities. At least until his injuries healed.

Her parents just happened to have a vacant guesthouse on their property.

The problem? He unnerved her. It was more than that tattoo and the circumstances surrounding his accident that reminded her of all she'd lost. No, her issue with Gus Coleman was shallower than all of that.

Even injured and borderline hypothermic, his rugged good looks had been impossible to ignore. She released a frustrated groan then focused on finishing the chart, determined to wrestle these feelings of attraction into submission. Abner had chosen Gus to be his best man in their wedding. Not that Abner would want her to be alone forever, but he'd also warned her on more than one occasion that Gus was trouble.

"Good morning." Dr. Calvert's voice filled the hospital corridor as she strode in, carrying a disposable carton filled with hot drinks from the Trading Post. "I asked the barista if she knew your favorite drink. Hope this is the right thing."

"Aw, thanks." Mia splayed her palm across her chest. "You didn't have to do that."

The middle-aged woman lifted one of the cups from the cardboard tray and set it in front of Mia. "I know a vanilla chai latte can't solve your water problem, but maybe it will take the edge off."

Mia froze, her hand extended halfway toward her favorite drink. "My what?"

Dr. Calvert tucked hair from her dark brown bob behind her ears. "Oh, dear. They haven't called you yet, have they?"

"Who?" Mia fumbled in her pocket for her phone. The screen was dark. Her battery had gone dead around 3:00 a.m., and she hadn't had time to borrow a charger. "Dr. Calvert, what is going on?"

"Your dad was in the Trading Post, picking up doughnuts and coffee. Apparently one of your sisters went by your house to borrow something and found water all over your floor."

No. A pathetic whimper left her lips.

"Broken pipes are the worst." Dr. Calvert scrunched her nose then reached for her drink. "Would you like to borrow my phone to call your parents?"

"N-no. I'll use the phone here." She reached for the landline receiver on the desk.

Dr. Calvert nodded. "Let me put my purse in a locker then you can give me a quick update and be on your way."

"Thank you." Mia punched Rylee's phone number into the keypad with trembling fingers.

Her youngest sister answered on the second ring. "Hello?"

"It's me. What's going on?"

"Hey, Mia. I guess you heard."

"Dr. Calvert just told me. I got called in to work around midnight."

"That explains why you didn't answer your phone," Rylee said.

"Do you know what happened?"

"A pipe broke or something. In your kitchen. I went by to borrow some of your cake pans. When you didn't answer the door, I used your spare key. That's when I saw the water. Don't worry, Asher and Dad are on it."

The tight knot lodged between her shoulders loosened a smidge. Dad and her brother-in-law would know what to do. She knew a few reputable contractors on the island, but rounding up someone to help while dealing with everything else going on in her life felt overwhelming.

"What's up with all those papers on your dining-room table?" Rylee asked. "Are you doing research about babies switched at birth?"

Panic welled in Mia's chest. "Please tell me you didn't touch anything."

"Relax. I didn't mess with your precious papers, all right? And you're welcome. If it weren't for me, your whole place would be flooded."

Mia blew out a long breath. "I'm sorry. I didn't mean to snap at you. Thanks for…getting involved."

"Are you coming by Mom and Dad's when your shift is over? I'm here with Mom. She wants to know."

"I'll be there as soon as I can."

"Good. See you soon."

"Wait." Mia twisted the phone's cord around her finger. "I need to ask you something."

"What's up?"

"Abner's childhood best friend was admitted during the night. He's stable, but he has significant injuries, and can't go back to Dillingham quite yet. Do you think Mom and Dad would mind if he lived in the guest cottage for a while?"

"Hang on, I'll ask."

Mia braced the phone between her ear and shoulder, then reached for her latte. Rylee and Mom's conversation filtered through the receiver in bits and pieces.

"Mom says bring him on by," Rylee said. "He can have the cottage and you can move back into your old bedroom."

Mia sputtered, choking on the first sip of her drink. "Wait. What?"

"Girl, your house is a mess. There's no way you can stay there. At least not right now."

Hot tears pricked her eyelids. Things just went from bad to worse. "Thanks for letting me know."

"You're welcome. Talk to you soon."

Mia hung up then pushed to her feet. Leaving her chai latte on the counter, she quickly swiped at her tears and trudged down the hall toward Gus's room. She could offer the guesthouse one more time. Maybe he'd admit that her advice was spot-on. Otherwise, Dr. Calvert would have to try and reason with him.

She hesitated, then rapped lightly on the door before pushing it open.

Gus sat up in bed, his breakfast tray on the table in front of him. Most of his meal sat untouched. He pressed the remote control and muted the volume on the television.

Mia moved to his bedside. She met his curious gaze with her own. Somehow his eyes were even more appealing this morning than usual. Maybe the blue squares in his hospital gown heightened the intensity. The blond stubble clinging to his jaw and his tousled hair added to his appeal. Not fair. Why did he get to look so handsome after surviving an accident? And why did she even notice? This was Gus.

She hadn't checked her appearance in several hours, but she imagined she looked ridiculous. Her fingers found their way to her messy bun. Probably had yesterday's mascara smeared on her face, too.

Nice. Not that it mattered. Much.

Gus plated his utensils. "What's up?"

"I checked with my parents. They said to bring you by whenever you're ready. The cottage is nice—I think you're going to like staying there."

Oh, brother. Now she was babbling. It wasn't like he was here on vacation. The man had nearly died.

A muscle in his cheek twitched. "That's a very generous offer, but I can't accept."

She linked her arms across her chest. Should've known he'd be obstinate about this. "Look, I know you want to get back home as soon as possible, but until your lung is healed and we're confident it won't collapse again, I strongly recommend that you stay here in Hearts Bay. Just for two weeks. We can order physical therapy, you can follow up with me or one of the physicians at the clinic, possibly get a referral for occupational therapy if necessary."

Gus's mouth flattened into a grim line. "I don't need therapy. All I really need is a new driver's license, a credit card and a job."

A twinge of empathy pushed past her annoyance. Poor guy. This was a lot to process. "While you're sorting all that out, why not stay in a comfortable home with people who can help you?"

She wanted to clamp her hand over her own mouth. What was wrong with her? He was a grown man. She didn't need to persuade him to stay. If he disregarded her professional opinion and suffered complications as a result, that was on him. She'd tried.

Sighing, Gus studied her, his expression unreadable. "Are you sure?"

"Sure that you need therapy?"

"Are you sure you're okay with me staying there?"

A charged silence filled the space between them. No, not sure at all. But it was the right thing to do. Besides, the news that he had a child had floored her. That meant his recovery was doubly important.

"My parents wouldn't have said yes if they weren't genuine," she said.

"All right." He slumped back against the pillow. "Thank you."

"You're welcome. I'll get the discharge paperwork started."

She strode from the room, her insides coiling into a hard knot. Having Gus around wouldn't be easy. Already, memories of Abner and their plans to build a house and raise a family in Hearts Bay had resurfaced. Her parents would welcome Gus into their home and fold him into their family's life. That's the kind of people they were. But she wouldn't. She couldn't. Abner had confided in her about Gus's irresponsible choices. He hadn't shown up when Abner needed him most. And as soon as Gus was well enough to travel, she'd help him get on the first flight back to Dillingham.

Chapter Two

Mia was right. He needed help. White-hot pain pierced Gus's chest. He stifled a groan and sank into the leather recliner in the Maddens' family room. Man, he felt like a toddler with Mia and her mother hovering, doing everything for him.

Flames crackled in the fireplace nearby and the familiar aroma of fresh cookies hung in the air. Their house was comfortable and welcoming. The opposite of a fishing boat. Maybe letting folks pamper him wouldn't be such a terrible thing.

"There you go." Mrs. Madden gently wedged another pillow between his elbow and torso. "Try to relax. I'll bring you some water. Do you need anything to eat?"

"No thanks." He forced out the words, hating that he probably sounded ungrateful. Mia and her family had taken him in when he deserved to be ignored. It was no secret that he'd been scheduled to be onboard with Charlie and Abner when they had lost their lives. Most people would've told him to get a motel room and suffer on his own.

But not the Maddens.

"Ring this bell if you need us." She pressed an old-school dinner bell into his hand. The kind someone would ring in a boardinghouse to summon their guests to dinner.

"Got it." Gus clamped his mouth shut and stole a glance at Mia, who was adding another log on the fire. She stood and faced him, her smooth brow furrowed. He might be injured but he was smart enough to know that if he summoned her with a bell, she would not be pleased.

"Now get some rest." Mrs. Madden patted his leg. "I'll be back to check on you in a few minutes. We need to make sure that fire's going strong."

"Mom, you need to take a nap." Mia looped her arm around Mrs. Madden's shoulders and tried to guide her away. "I'll come back to check on him. After he rests, I'll get Dad to help him move to the guesthouse."

Mrs. Madden ignored her daughter and pulled a well-loved quilt from the back of the sofa then draped it over him. "We're glad to have you, Gus."

"Thank you. For everything."

"You're welcome."

"Wait." Gus fought against the heavy sensation pulling him under. "Before you go, may I borrow a phone, please? I need to call my sister."

Mia pursed her lips then pulled her phone from her pocket. "Sure, but try not to overexert yourself. You really need to rest. Besides, your pain medication is going to kick in and you'll probably start to feel drowsy."

Huh. So she really did care. Her all-business attitude in the hospital had made him wonder if she even liked him. He couldn't help but smile at her attentiveness. "Make it quick, is what you're saying."

She didn't return his smile. Not even a smirk. "Exactly."

She handed over the phone without another word.

"Thanks." He took the device, noting the screen featured a gorgeous picture of the ocean off the coast of the island on a brilliant sunny day. His own lock-screen photo had been one of Poppy holding her favorite pink sippy cup and grinning at the camera. Man, he missed his little girl.

Mia and her mother left the room, speaking in hushed tones.

He shifted in the chair, trying to find a comfortable position, but no matter how he moved, the stabbing pain in his chest persisted. That stupid tube stitched to his chest and snaking into his lung made him the most uncomfortable. He'd certainly comply with whatever he needed to do to get that thing removed.

The pain medication clouded his thinking, like a dense fog surrounding his vessel when he was out at sea. Gritting his teeth, he tried to resist the fatigue. He had to talk to his sister and let her know he was okay. Well, mostly okay. Then he'd get in touch with Liesel and let her know he wouldn't be back in Dillingham anytime soon. They'd have to work out an agreement for her to keep Poppy until he recovered.

That was not going to be an easy conversation.

His arm felt like it weighed a thousand pounds as he tried to brace the phone against his leg and jabbed at the icon to call Carina. He'd broken bones before, but nothing quite this severe. It took all his effort to lift the phone to his ear. Maybe he should've tried a video call instead. But honestly, he didn't want Carina to see him like this. If he allowed her to get an accurate picture of his condition, she'd only worry more than she already did.

He'd be fine. He'd find his way forward, just like he always did.

Carina answered on the second ring. "Hello?"

"Hey. It's me."

"Oh, Gus, I'm so glad you called."

Oh, no. Was she crying? "Are you all right?"

"Where are you?" Her voice quivered. "I heard about the accident, and I've been worried sick."

"I'm sorry." He tried to breathe through a fresh wave of pain. "I should've called sooner."

She sniffed. "Are you on your way home?"

"Not exactly."

"Hang on."

A child crying in the background interrupted their conversation.

Carina sighed. "My kids are grumpy."

"I won't keep you long."

"You're not bothering me, Gus. I need to know what happened. Let me get them a snack then we can talk more."

Gus fought back a fresh wave of pain and listened to the familiar sound of Carina doling out snacks and refilling sippy cups. He couldn't wait to get home and handle the ordinary tasks of everyday life with Poppy.

"There." Carina returned to their conversation. "That will buy me a few minutes. You were about to tell me where you're at right now."

He drew a ragged breath. "Hearts Bay on

Orca Island. The Coast Guard brought us here because it had the closest hospital."

"When will you be discharged?"

"Here's the thing…" Gus hesitated. He hated to tell her this, but he couldn't keep the truth from her, either. "The kind of injury I have, a punctured lung, means that flying is dangerous."

"Yikes. You sound like you're in a lot of pain, too. I want you to focus on getting well."

"I will, but if I can't get back to Dillingham soon, I'm not going to be able to pick up Poppy."

"Uh-oh."

"Liesel is going to be so annoyed. She has zero patience for disruptions in her well-ordered plans."

Man, he was dreading that conversation.

"Let me know how I can help."

A piercing shriek in the background made Gus wince. "It's my responsibility to reach out to Liesel and explain what happened, even though I know she'll have a fit. Besides, I can't ask you to watch Poppy. You've got two little kids to take care of already."

"And one on the way."

Oh, wow. "Congratulations. Right? This is a good thing."

"Well, I mean, we had talked about having more kids, but three under the age of five is going to be a bit much, even for me. And I had preeclampsia last time, so the doctor's already talking about keeping an eye on my blood pressure."

His breath hitched. *Please, Lord, don't let anything happen to Carina.* He'd be in a world of hurt without his sister. "How are you feeling?"

"Not great, but I'll get by."

"This really stinks. You didn't need any extra stress, especially when your husband's away." His brother-in-law worked in the oil fields. He was gone for two weeks at a time in northern Alaska.

"Gus, please don't worry about me. I'll be fine, and so will Poppy. If Liesel can't adjust her work schedule and she needs childcare, please let her know I'm available."

"I know you'll help, but you shouldn't have to."

"Why not? That's what family is for."

"You've stepped up for me way more than I ever have for you." Wow, he hadn't meant to admit that out loud.

"Don't be ridiculous. I'd take a bullet for you— you know that. Please try to remember Liesel's behavior is not your responsibility to manage. You were in a horrible accident. That's not something you can control. Do not feel guilty about this, Gus. Don't."

He didn't have the strength to argue. He and Carina had been down this road before. Their father had been horrible to her. His deviant behavior had eventually landed him in prison, but by then it was too late. The damage had been done, and Gus would never forgive himself for not being able to protect her.

"I'll call you as often as I can. I don't have any ID or my phone. None of that stuff survived."

"But you survived. That's what matters."

"So did the rest of our guys, and I'm thankful. It was brutal out there." He shuddered at the mental images that flashed through his head again. "I was told that I can't fly for two weeks. If Liesel will accept your help, Poppy might need to stay with you for more than just a weekend."

"I can handle it. Jeb will chip in when he's here."

"You shouldn't have to take care of Poppy for me. That's not fair."

"Then we'll pray that Liesel will have some grace and be willing to understand your situation."

Yeah, but what if she didn't?

"If you're injuries are that serious, who is taking care of you?"

"Mia, Abner's former fiancée. Her parents are letting me stay with them."

"Oh, is that right?" He could sense that she was smiling. "Good to know."

"Stop. It's not what you think."

"So she isn't the beautiful one with auburn hair and gorgeous green eyes?"

He grunted.

"I've seen her picture. She's quite lovely, as I recall. I'm glad she and her family are willing to help."

"Me, too," he mumbled, fighting back another wave of fatigue.

"I'll let you go. The kids need to go down for their naps."

"I'll be in touch. I'm so sorry."

"Stop apologizing. You didn't do anything wrong. I love you, Gustav."

"I love you, too." As he ended the call, Carina's words swam in his fuzzy brain. He had to figure out how to get to his little girl.

Pain and exhaustion overwhelmed his determination to stay awake. His eyelids grew heavy. He struggled to sift through his convoluted thoughts. This lying around waiting for his body to heal was the pits. He should call Liesel, but he didn't trust himself to have a civil conversation. She'd probably accuse him of lying about his condition, anyway.

Oh, how he loathed feeling helpless. It stirred up painful childhood memories. Grim flashbacks when his father had harmed Carina, and Gus had been powerless to intervene.

"This is the last bag." Rylee gestured to the purple duffel bag she'd lugged from Mia's bedroom. "Except for the papers on the table that you told me I couldn't touch."

Mia sighed and rubbed the grit from her eyes. She was going on almost eighteen hours of being awake, but she couldn't rest, not until she was out of her waterlogged house and settled in her parents' guest room. Even if that meant frequent interactions with Gus Coleman.

"You can touch the papers. It's fine. I mean, I had to tell you about it sometime, right?"

Rylee's eyes widened. "Tell me about what?"

"Come on, let's go outside." Mia gathered the documents, shoved them in the plastic bin, clipped the lid in place and led her sister out of the house. Pulling the door shut to drown out the sound of the industrial dryers and fans, she reveled in the peaceful silence of the outdoors. Last night's fierce storm had passed. Now the afternoon sun glistened off the fresh snow blanketing her yard.

They stood on the porch. Concern filled Rylee's eyes. "What's going on?"

Mia clutched the plastic bin tighter. If only there was an easy way to share this. "A woman named Lexi Thomas who lives in Georgia sent me a message on social media before Christmas. She said she has proof that we were switched at birth when we were newborns."

Rylee gasped then clapped her hand over her mouth.

"Hard to believe, right? I was skeptical at first. Still kind of am, to be honest. She's done her research, though. She also said someone on the event planning committee reached out and told her about the commemoration we're having in May."

"Oh, my." Rylee squeezed her arm. "How are you doing? That's a lot to process."

"Ironically, I'm supposed to be on the planning committee for the commemoration, but now that I've heard from Lexi, that's the last thing I want to do. I can only imagine the gossip, the pitying stares." She shuddered. "No thank you."

"This information will be tough to keep under wraps. If it's really true." Rylee fiddled with the strap on the duffel bag she'd carried out. "I hate to ask, but have you spoken with Mom and Dad about all this?"

Mia turned and walked toward her car. "I was planning to. Mom's aplastic anemia is getting worse. She needs a bone-marrow transplant. I'm worried about how the stress of this news will impact her health."

"I don't blame you for feeling conflicted." Rylee trailed after her.

"It's hard to know what to do. None of us are a match for Mom. What if Lexi is?" She swallowed against the tightness in her throat as she opened the hatch of her SUV and slid the bin inside. Rylee had already helped her pack two suitcases full of clothing and another box of books and essential toiletries. The guys had come from the water-restoration company and sopped up the mess, and friends had brought fans to dry out the moisture. It was going to be a long process to clean up the damage and renovate her soggy kitchen.

"I can't quite wrap my mind around the concept that she exists, much less figure out if she's the donor we've been hoping for." Rylee wedged the bag in next to the bin. "Do you think Mom and Dad know anything about Lexi or babies getting switched? I mean, there must be a mistake. Right?"

"The only explanation I can come up with is someone accidentally sent babies home with the wrong mothers. Now, thirty-five years later, we're all going to celebrate and reunite parents with their real daughters."

Rylee's eyes widened.

Okay, that sounded way too cynical. She buried her face in her hands. "I'm sorry."

"You don't have to apologize." Rylee gently offered a side hug. "We'll figure this out. Together."

Mia patted her sister's back then quickly pulled away. "I'm exhausted. I have no filter right now. I need to get some sleep." Gus's injuries and her grueling night in the ER treating him and his crewmates had done her in. They'd all survived, but their grave conditions had pushed her and the hospital's meager staff to their limit.

"What does Lexi want?"

"She wants to come here. I mean, I can't blame her. You guys are her real family."

"No." Rylee shook her head, then slammed the SUV's hatch closed. "That's not true. We're not her family. I mean, maybe genetically, but Mia, you're our sister. You're a Madden."

"But what if I'm not?" Mia whispered, blinking back tears. "Am I supposed to go to Georgia and meet these people who are really my mom and dad? Do I have brothers and sisters? Am I supposed to step aside while Lexi comes here, and you all welcome her home?"

Now she sounded like a monster. She wrapped her arms around her torso, wishing that she wasn't even saying these words out loud.

"Those are all excellent questions. I wish I had answers." Rylee sniffed and dabbed at the moisture trickling from her eyes. "Thank you for trusting me with this. Come on. Let's get you settled at the house."

"You drive." Mia handed over the keys then trudged around to the passenger's side and climbed in. They rode in silence until Rylee parked in their parents' driveway. Once they got out, Mia hauled her luggage from the vehicle to the front door. Gus was inside, probably asleep. She pushed open the front door, wincing when the hinges squeaked. She set down the suitcases and quietly stepped inside. Rylee followed her carrying a box and a duffel bag.

Mia gestured for Rylee to be quiet and pointed toward the family room, then tiptoed in to check on him. The recliner sat empty. The blankets had been pushed aside. What was he doing up? She'd specifically told him to rest and avoid overexertion. What was the point of giving her professional opinion if he was only going to ignore her?

The deep tenor of his voice floated from the kitchen, followed by her mother's laughter. Mom was supposed to be resting, too. Irritation simmered inside. Of course. He was probably in there charming his way into her good graces. Same old Gus. Only thinking of himself.

Time to put a stop to that. She strode into the kitchen, anger burning hotter with every step.

"Oh, hi, sweetie." Her mother smiled from her usual spot at the kitchen table. The dark circles under her eyes and bruises along her forearms made Mia want to burst into tears. Again. They had to find a donor match. And soon.

"What's wrong?" Her mother's tone grew sober. "You look tired. Why don't you lie down?"

Mia bit back a frustrated groan. Everything about this scenario was backward.

Gus sat across from Mom, an empty bowl and plate in front of him. His eyes found Mia's and her insides dipped and swayed. *No, no, huh-uh. We're not doing this.* Just because he was handsome didn't mean he could manipulate her.

Mom cleared her throat. "How's the house?"

The house? Mia glanced at her mother. Oh, right. "It's okay. Drying out."

"You must be exhausted," Mom said. "Would you like something to eat?"

Rylee's wet boots squeaked on the hardwood floor as she brought more of Mia's belongings inside. "I'll grab the rest." She gave Mia a long look, then gazed at Gus, before hurrying back out to the car.

Mia pulled out a chair at the end of the table—the one farthest away from Gus—and sank into it. "Please stay off your feet, Mom. I'll get something in a minute." She slid her gaze to Gus. "You must be feeling better, since you're up and eating."

"I've had better days." A crimson scab had formed over a laceration on his cheek. He rubbed his fingers over the stubble thickening on his jaw, which somehow only added to his rugged good looks. "Sorry to hear about your house. What happened?"

"Broken pipe, I think." She stifled a yawn. "I'll have to stay here until things get cleaned up and the repairs are finished."

Gus's eyebrows raised but he didn't say anything.

"I'm sorry you two are both dealing with such difficult situations." Mom offered Mia an empathetic glance. "Gus was just telling me how difficult it is for him to be away from his daughter, Poppy, while he's stuck recovering here. I told him we'd be glad to have Poppy, too."

"Mom." Mia glared at her. "You can't. It's too much stress on you to add a toddler to the mix right now."

Eyes fixed on the table, Gus winced then shifted in his chair. An awkward silence filled the kitchen.

Mom studied her, something indecipherable flickering across her face. Then she averted her eyes and gently placed her hand on Gus's arm. "Pretend she never said that. She worries too much. We'd be glad to have your little girl stay here with us. Can I get you some more soup?"

Warmth crawled up Mia's neck as she pushed back her chair then strode from the room. At the end of the hall, she stormed into the guest bedroom and slammed the door.

Real mature, Mia.

Dark spots peppered her vision as she flopped on her back in the middle of the queen-size bed. She'd done everything she could to help her parents find a solution to Mom's complicated health issues. Now that they had a diagnosis and the specialist in Seattle had recommended a treatment plan, Mom had resisted every attempt to take the next step. What was she thinking? Didn't she want to get well?

Mia surrendered to the fatigue that had dogged her all day. She'd rest and then regroup. Because there was no way she'd let aplastic anemia win this fight.

Chapter Three

"That went well." Gus closed the app and set aside the tablet. Scrubbing his hand across his face, he tipped back his head and stared at the ceiling.

Mr. Madden had come out to the guest-house to check on him early this morning and helped him relocate to the recliner in the family room. Then Mr. and Mrs. Madden had left the house after loaning him a device so he could call Liesel. He'd summoned his courage after breakfast, hoping a video call would give him an opportunity to see Poppy.

Instead, Liesel had refused his request. She didn't express even an ounce of empathy for his situation, either. Shocker.

No matter how many times he asked, his ex-wife refused to budge. She insisted that if Poppy saw him on the screen but couldn't be with him, she'd get upset.

"Ridiculous," he muttered. Carina had used FaceTime at least twice when she'd babysat Poppy for him. His precious little girl had smiled and laughed the whole time. He'd even read a short book to her once and she'd listened happily from Carina's lap.

He'd learned the sad reality that from Liesel's perspective, she was always right, and he was always wrong. How had they fallen in love, married and had a child?

Lord, help me heal quickly so I can get home to Poppy.

It was a prayer he'd offered several times already, and one he'd whisper until he was cleared to travel. When he'd relayed Carina's offer to babysit Poppy since he couldn't get home for his next parenting visit, Liesel's pinched expression had indicated her disapproval. But she hadn't lobbed any thinly veiled threats at him. One small sliver of sunshine in their otherwise dismal conversation. They'd ended the call without getting into an argument. He couldn't shake a vague sense of unease, though. The woman was a well-respected police officer, and he didn't doubt that she was a decent mother, but, man, she was a challenge to deal with. He'd planned to tell Liesel about Mrs. Madden's offer for him to have Poppy visit Hearts Bay, but after Mia made it clear she wasn't on board with the idea, he hadn't mentioned it to his ex-wife.

The sound of someone making coffee in the kitchen got his attention. He tried to ease forward and push to a standing position, but the pain in his chest drove him back to the cushions with a muffled groan.

"Gus?" Mia padded into the room. "Are you all right?"

"Yeah." He slumped sideways on his uninjured elbow. "I just need a minute."

"Did you get any sleep?" She stifled a yawn behind her hand.

"Some." He let his gaze wander from her bright eyes to her long hair tumbling over her blue sweatshirt, to her gray joggers and moccasin-style slippers. "How about you?"

She glanced at her watch. "About fourteen hours apparently. That might be a new record."

He forced himself to sit up again. The pain made him suck in a breath.

"Here, let me help you." She moved closer and braced his elbow and back as he pushed to his feet.

"Thank you."

"Do you know where my parents are?"

"Your dad took your mom to the doctor. She has a fever."

Mia's eyes rounded. "You're kidding."

Gus shook his head. "They left about twenty minutes ago."

She whirled away. "I need to find my phone. Why didn't they wake me up?"

He squeezed his eyes shut. Mr. Madden warned him that Mia would react this way. Said not to panic, either. He followed her into the kitchen. "They asked me to tell you they'd text as soon as they had more information."

"That's what they always say," she called from down the hall.

Gus stole a glance at the coffee maker gurgling on the counter nearby. Rylee had dropped by earlier with a bag of clothes from the local sporting-goods store. She'd helped him with breakfast. He'd eaten a banana and drank the smoothie she'd made. He'd politely declined the coffee Mr. Madden had offered, though. The stuff had looked dark as midnight and strong enough to curl his hair.

The pleasing aroma of fresh coffee was hard to resist now. Especially if he could sit with Mia and savor a cup. He shook off the thought. Given the way she'd stormed out of the kitchen yesterday and her awareness of her mother's health, he doubted she'd be sticking around long enough to eat or drink anything.

She strode back into the kitchen, phone in hand. "Would you like some coffee?"

Well, how about that. "Please."

"Have a seat." She gestured toward the table then moved past him. "I'll bring it to you. Cream or sugar?"

"Both, please." He managed to sit down in the wooden chair without howling in pain. The prospect of coffee with Mia was enough to keep him from stumbling back to the guesthouse and succumbing to sleep.

Mia joined him a few minutes later and set two large steaming mugs on the table between them. She added a pitcher of cream, a bowl of sugar and a plate with two Danishes covered in plastic wrap.

"Let me get some plates and forks." She brought those to the table then pulled out the chair opposite his and sat down. "Did my dad feed you anything before they left?"

"Your sister Rylee did." He gestured to his new plaid button-down and black sweatpants. "Brought me some new clothes, too."

"Aww, that was sweet." Mia added cream and sugar to her coffee, then glanced at her phone. "My dad's recent text says they're waiting to see the doctor now."

"If you don't mind my asking, what's going on with your mom? I would have never agreed to come here if I'd known she had a serious health problem."

Mia's mouth twitched. "Did you have some-place else you could go? A better offer I don't know about?"

"Very funny. No, of course not. And I appreciate everything your family's doing for me. I feel like I'm imposing, though."

"My mom has a rare condition called aplastic anemia. She needs a donor for a stem-cell transplant." Her spoon clinked against the side of the mug as she stirred. "We haven't been able to find a viable match."

"That's awful. I'm so sorry. What are you going to do?"

Fierce determination sparked in her eyes. "We're going to keep looking. I'm not going to give up."

Of course not. Despite the sobering news, he couldn't help but admire her attitude. Mia didn't strike him as the kind of person who let obstacles stand in her way. "How do you go about finding a potential donor? Is there a test?"

"Mom has already been tested. It's all about finding someone who has similar protein molecules. The more markers two people have that are alike, the happier the immune system will be with the donation. So far none of us are a match."

"Next you'll move on to testing people who aren't blood relatives? Isn't there a list of potential donors on a registry?"

"Ideally there will be a small pool of donors who are potential matches." Mia hesitated, then tugged the plastic wrap from the pastries. "But there's been a bit of a plot twist."

Gus carefully sipped his coffee and waited for her to continue.

"Just before Christmas, I received a message through social media from a woman named Lexi who claimed she and I were switched at birth."

"Oh, wow." He lowered his mug to the table. "Do you think she's telling the truth?"

"She seems to have proof. Maybe she did one of those online DNA tests. I haven't asked yet. Anyway, she wants to come to Hearts Bay and meet all of us."

"And how do you feel about that?"

Mia lifted one shoulder then sliced her fork through a corner of the Danish. "I'm struggling. That kind of news really creates a lot of turmoil in a family. My parents don't need any more stress right now."

He winced. In his condition, he was adding to everyone's workload and stress level.

Her cheeks flushed. "I—I didn't mean you."

"Oh, but you did." He helped himself to a pastry, half expecting Mia to tell him he should watch his sugar and processed carbohydrates.

She hesitated, her fork halfway to her mouth. "I need to apologize for my behavior yesterday.

When you told my mother about your daughter, and she offered to help. I was rude. I'm sorry."

"It's not a problem. I understand. You're only looking out for your mother's best interests."

"But that's no excuse for being unkind or stomping out of the room like a child. If you need help getting your daughter here, we can figure out how to make those arrangements."

Her kindness surprised him. He opened his mouth. Closed it. His thoughts churned. He couldn't keep taking advantage of the Maddens. No matter how desperately he wanted to see his daughter. There had to be something he could offer in return. "I'll agree to those arrangements on one condition."

She studied him. "What's that?"

"You let me test to see if I'm a donor match."

Her fork clattered to the table. "Gus, no."

"Why not? Isn't it just a blood test or a cheek swab or something?"

"At first, it's pretty straightforward. Usually a cheek swab. But if you're a match and you agree to donate, then the process is more involved. Probably a physical exam, more bloodwork, a lot of needles, an overnight hospital stay, recovery time—"

"It can't be more challenging than what I just went through. Minus the brutal storm." His attempt at humor fell flat. Impulsively, he reached out and covered her hand with his own. "Your family has been gracious when most people would've left me to rot in a motel room somewhere. Let me do this for you. Please."

The warmth of his strong hand blanketing hers sent a delightful tingle careening up her arm. She gazed into his eyes. This was not the same Gus Coleman that Abner had warned her about. That Gus cared about having a good time, and very little about the needs of others. He'd certainly never insisted on being the next in line to make a potential life-saving donation.

She gently extracted her hand from his. "I can't ask you to do that."

"You didn't ask," his deep voice rumbled. "I offered."

She pushed aside her plate. Her craving for a sweet pastry had suddenly vanished. "I want to make sure you fully understand what you're getting yourself into. We can do the initial testing here, but after that you'll have to travel to Anchorage. As we've already discussed, in your current condition that's not possible."

"I won't be in this condition forever, though." One corner of his mouth tipped up in a half smile. "Right?"

Her eyes slid to the curve of his full lips and her two-faced heart turned against her, beating faster. Argh, why did he have to be handsome and persuasive?

"Mia?" Gus prompted. "With time and therapy, I'm going to get better, right?"

"Yes, of course." She reached for her coffee. "I—I was thinking about…your offer. I don't know what to say."

"Easy. Just say 'sounds like a plan. Let's get started.'"

"I'm not exaggerating, Gus. Sometimes they harvest bone marrow from your pelvis. You might have an adverse reaction and need to stay in the hospital for a few days."

Again, he shrugged one muscular shoulder. He had to be in so much pain. How could he possibly volunteer to undergo an additional procedure when he hadn't even recovered from his current injuries?

"I'm a crab fisherman. There's always risk and agony associated with my lifestyle."

She tapped her fingernails against the side of her mug. He'd dismissed every single one of her concerns. "I don't know how we'll follow through on our part. Getting your daughter here, I mean."

Oh, boy. Was this really happening? Sure, her sisters had kids and her parents were always happy when children visited, but that wasn't the same as having one move in. If she roped Rylee into helping, they could probably handle a toddler. But what if Poppy was high-maintenance? Or she got sick? Gus could barely take care of himself. They'd have to do a lion's share of the work until he was well.

"I can tell you're about to freak out." He carefully sliced his fork through the Danish. "Slow down. We'll take this one step at a time."

"Obviously, a toddler can't fly alone, so someone would have to bring her here from Dillingham."

"Mia." He shot her a look. "You're overthinking this."

Easy for him to say. It was her job to think through all the details. Especially the ones other people hadn't bothered to consider yet. She took another sip of her coffee, letting the warm sweet liquid slide down her throat as her mind raced.

Her phone hummed on the table. She leaned forward and glanced at the screen. Hopefully this was an update from her dad. Instead, a new message from Lexi greeted her. She couldn't stifle her groan. Seeing Lexi's name made Mia's palms sweat. What was she supposed say to this woman who held the power to upend her whole world?

"Bad news?" Gus asked.

"It's Lexi again. She really wants to come to Alaska. There's this big event in the spring to commemorate our birthdays. There were eight

of us born that day, right after a volcanic eruption. It's been thirty-five years and Hearts Bay
wants to acknowledge the event. I volunteered
to be on the planning committee, but now I—"

"You're not interested."

This time, Gus finished her sentence.

She wrinkled her nose. "Is that terrible?"

He shook his head. "Given your mother's condition, you shouldn't think twice about stepping
away from the committee. And you don't owe
anyone an explanation, either."

"But what am I supposed to tell Lexi?" Her
voice faltered. She pressed her palm to her forehead. "That her biological mother needs a stem-
cell transplant? That's information a person in
Lexi's position should know. But it also feels slimy
and manipulative. Like I'm only connecting with
her because we want to see her protein markers."

"You're being too hard on yourself. If your
mother was healthy, wouldn't you have responded to Lexi's message?"

"Of course. Although to be honest, I'm stalling. I did acknowledge that I'd read her messages, but beyond that I've been too shocked
and confused to tell my parents about her. Or
tell Lexi about Mom's aplastic anemia."

Gus studied her over the rim of his mug.
"What if telling Lexi everything means your
mother finds a donor?"

"Then everyone would get what they want," she whispered.

Except me.

She averted her gaze. Shame heated her skin. This wasn't the time to be selfish. But her conversation with Gus forced her to confront the ugly thoughts she'd tried unsuccessfully to banish. Mom desperately needed a stem-cell transplant and there was a slim chance Lexi might be a match. If Lexi visited, she'd get to meet her biological family, which seemed to be the desire of her heart.

But Mia would be left to deal with the fallout.

Was she putting her family at risk by allowing this stranger into their lives? What if Lexi wasn't a match but could still prove she was genetically a Madden? Then Mia was going to be pushed out. Made an outsider. A person who didn't belong in her own family any longer.

"Do you want to connect with your biological parents at all?"

"I don't know." Mia folded her napkin into a neat square. Lexi hadn't said much about them. Did they have any desire to meet? What if she reached out and they rejected her? That would break her heart. All over again.

Not that she'd share *that* with Gus. She'd already been way too honest.

"Lexi should be a part of the commemoration. Not only is it our birthday, it's our origin story. She's clearly eager to fill in the missing pieces of this puzzle she's uncovered. But I'm still worried about what her arrival here will mean for the people I love."

"I'm not the best guy to be quoting Bible verses, but I know one thing for sure." Gus managed to eat another bite of Danish before pushing aside his plate. "I'm supposed to tell you to pray about this. To ask God to help you make the right choice."

Oh, wow. Add that to the list of things she never thought she'd hear Abner's best friend say.

"The right thing to do is to invite Lexi here to meet everyone. But first I have to tell my family that she exists."

"I'll do whatever I can to help." Gus smiled weakly. "I'm here for you."

She looked away, flustered by his kindness.

He winced as he shifted in his chair.

"You need to lie down." She stood and started clearing the table. "When did you take your last dose of medication?"

"I'm supposed to wait another hour," he grunted.

"I've got to get going. I need to get over to the clinic and see what's going on with my mom. Will you be okay by yourself for a little while?"

"Yep."

"I'll help you get back to the guesthouse." She put the dishes and cups in the sink, then morphed into caretaker mode. It was easier that way. Then she didn't have to think about how Gus and Abner had been closer than brothers. Or how these complicated feelings for her late fiancé's best friend were clouding her judgment. She'd always hold a special place in her heart for Abner. Staying single for the rest of her life because he'd died too soon wasn't what she truly wanted.

Yet falling for his best friend was not an option.

She needed someone who provided stability and came home every night. Someone whose job didn't require going toe-to-toe with life-threatening storms. Sure, Gus was a surprisingly great listener. He'd shared some helpful insights and his offer to get tested to see if he was a donor match was incredibly generous, but he was still a crab fisherman.

Helping him get well so he could leave Hearts Bay and get back to Poppy had to be the focus of their interactions moving forward. Because if she wasn't careful, those piercing blue eyes and his calming presence would just keep reeling her in. And she wouldn't allow herself to love another man that might surrender his life to the sea.

Chapter Four

I'm here for you.

His foolish offer to Mia still rang in his ears a day later.

What had he been thinking? Gus had noted the disbelief flashing in her eyes. Sensed the judgment in her ramrod-straight posture. There was no way she trusted him enough to help resolve her mother's complicated health issues.

Gus finished his last set of ten repetitions. Squeezing a foam ball made him feel like a child. He had a tube protruding from his chest and couldn't lift his arm. Basically useless. He had no business trying to donate anything from his broken body.

"Great work, Gus." Jessica, his way-too-chipper physical therapist, glanced up from her post behind her mobile workstation. Her wide smile disguised her ability to push him to his physical limits. Their first session had been grueling.

"Thanks," he said, struggling to layer his flannel button-down over his T-shirt. Quite the feat when he only had use of one arm. Not that he'd admit that to her. The last thing he wanted or needed was another person swooping in and helping him get dressed. Or fed. Or driven around town.

Yeah, okay, so maybe he needed to put attitude change on his list of to-dos.

"Activities of daily living are going to be a challenge." Jessica's keyboard clicked under her fingers. "Have you considered asking your provider to prescribe occupational therapy?"

He gritted his teeth. "I appreciate your input. I'll see what Mia has to say."

Right on cue, he heard her speaking to the receptionist around the corner in the lobby. He managed to pull his flannel button-down over one arm, but left the other side dangling because of his stupid sling.

"See you next time," Jessica said.

"Can't wait," he called over his shoulder as he walked slowly toward Mia. Every single one of his extremities ached. But he couldn't give up. He had to push through the pain. For Poppy.

Mia slanted a look his way. "How did it go?"

"Meh." He tried to shrug, which sent a piercing arrow of pain zinging along his collarbone. Wincing, he followed her out of the clinic.

Her keys jangled and snow crunched under her boots as she strode to her SUV. He squinted against the bright sunlight. She walked like she was angry. Quick strides, choppy steps and arms swinging. Was he supposed to ask what was bothering her? He ambled to the passenger side of the vehicle.

She stood on the driver's side with her door open, but didn't get in. "Do you need help with your seat belt?"

Yes. "No."

She didn't even bother to get in the car. As if she knew he was going to need her help. Man, that was aggravating. And who knew one session of physical therapy would hurt so much? He'd squeezed that stupid ball about thirty times, walked on a treadmill for eight minutes and pushed his arm against a doorframe. Isometrics or something. For a guy who was used to working almost around the clock hauling crab pots in freezing rain, he'd suddenly turned into a wimp.

Mia circled around the front of the vehicle then opened his door. She waited until he'd maneuvered into the passenger seat. Reaching around him with his seat belt, she leaned so close her hair tickled his nose. He breathed in the scent of something floral. Appealing. The buckle clicked into place, and she pulled away much too soon for his liking.

"There you go." She stepped back and closed the door.

He intentionally stared straight ahead and trained his gaze on the clinic's entrance so he wouldn't track her as she walked back around to the driver's side. It had been a long time since he'd enjoyed the company of a woman. His relationship with Liesel had gone south quickly, then imploded. Almost every conversation they had turned into an argument. He'd been so jaded and discouraged after his marriage failed that he hadn't bothered dating anyone.

Mia slid behind the wheel and slammed the door with more force than necessary. He snuck a glance out of the corner of his eye. She had on a puffy green jacket the color of a Sitka spruce tree, black jeans and lace-up winter boots. She'd twisted her reddish-brown hair into a long braid that fell over her shoulder when she turned to grab her seat belt. Man, she was stunning.

And now he really felt like a dirtbag for being attracted to his dead best friend's girl. But it had been almost four years. She was still single. Abner never would've expected Mia to spend the rest of her life alone, pining for him. If the situation had been reversed, Abner would not have remained single for the rest of his life, much less four years.

She dropped her keys in the console, then

pushed the button to start the engine and blew out a long breath.

"Do you want to grab some coffee and talk about whatever's bothering you?"

A muscle in her cheek twitched as she checked behind her, then shifted into Reverse.

He swallowed against the dryness in his mouth. Oy, he was terrible at this. He used to be so smooth with the ladies. Then again, that version of him never would've asked out a woman for something as basic as coffee.

Mia glanced over at him, her eyes questioning.

"Or not? We can go back to the house if you've got stuff to do."

"I thought we were going to help you get a new driver's license." She drove toward the exit at the edge of the parking lot then eased to a stop. "The DMV's close by."

"I borrowed your parents' computer and checked the website. They aren't open yet. Besides, if it's okay with you, I'll just request a new license online and have it mailed here to your family's address."

"That works." She looked both ways then turned onto the street. "Ever been to the Trading Post?"

"What's that?"

"My favorite coffee place."

He tried to hide a smile. Maybe he wasn't so bad at asking her to do something fun after all. "Let's go."

She drove a few blocks, then turned onto Main Street and crept along, craning her neck to check for a parking space. He saw the sign advertising the Trading Post. All the spots in front of the modest shop were taken, so she circled the block and found a space in an empty lot behind the building.

He climbed out of the vehicle, grimacing in pain. This was a terrible idea. He should go home, take his pain medication and have a long nap. Home. Funny how that word so easily slipped into his mind. Sure, he'd spent some time here over the years, but he'd never considered Hearts Bay or Orca Island to be a place he associated with home. Guess the Maddens had made him feel welcome. Not that it mattered. He couldn't stay here long-term. He had to get back to Dillingham and see Poppy. And hopefully land a job on another boat before crabbing season ended.

Mia's phone rang. She hesitated, then pulled it from her pocket and glanced at the screen. "It's my dad. I have to take this."

"No worries." Gus turned away to give her privacy. Since he'd lost his wallet and his phone, he didn't have a single dollar in his possession to pay for anything. He opened the door to the coffee shop and stepped inside. The aromas of fresh coffee and sweet pastries greeted him. He hovered against the wall and surveyed the wood beams overhead, then saw a comfortable couch and two armchairs arranged near the gas fireplace and framed artwork of Alaskan scenery adorning the walls. Conversations filtered through the warm air. Customers mingled around tables that dotted the café area. This place had a vibe that fit Mia. He wasn't one to sit still for long, but if sipping coffee in a cozy shop got Mia talking, then he was all for it.

The door opened and she came in, sending a wave of cool air swirling around them. Those stunning green eyes met his gaze. Her crimped brow made his stomach clench.

Uh-oh. "Everything okay?"

"My dad received a phone call from a woman named Liesel." She tucked a loose strand of hair behind her ear. "She's trying to reach you. Says she has news about your sister and your daughter."

Oh, no. His pulse thrummed. What had happened to Carina and Poppy?

"Oh, Mia, I'm so glad I ran into you." An older woman with curly salt-and-pepper hair blocked their path to the front counter. She was holding a disposable cup of coffee and a white paper bag. "Why aren't you returning my calls? We need to sit down and finalize the plans for the commemoration. If we don't, it will be next to impossible to schedule the chair-and-table rental."

Mia's sharp intake of breath sent his hand instinctively to the small of her back. Who was this woman? Her pushy comment raised his hackles. Challenging her wide-eyed gaze with his most frigid stare, he stepped closer to Mia. "If you'll excuse us, please. We're dealing with a family emergency. Mia will have to get back to you another time."

The woman's mouth tightened, but he didn't give her another second to speak. Gritting his teeth against the pain radiating through his torso like a live wire, he guided Mia toward the back of the line. He'd probably overstepped. It seemed like she was about to tell him to back off. Somehow, the fierce need to protect her had trampled all other thoughts. Including his own mental gymnastics about how he didn't belong here and couldn't stay on the island. A vague message from Liesel was a stark reminder of the complicated reality waiting for him back home.

He dropped his hand from Mia's back as she stepped up to order, her expression unreadable. Yeah, he'd botched the whole situation. But somebody needed to intervene. Besides, putting a stop to thoughtless comments wasn't exactly evidence of a long-term commitment. He'd only done what any decent human would have.

Right?

Mia's hands trembled as she pulled her debit card from her purse and paid for their coffee and doughnuts. Curious stares boring into her back made her eager to leave. She fought back a smile. Plenty of people in Hearts Bay had wanted to tell Mrs. Lovell to mind her business. Her meddling grated on people's nerves and occasionally caused an avalanche of heartache. Gus had probably been one of the first to deny her what she wanted.

"I'm sorry if I overstepped." He leaned toward her ear and kept his voice low.

The warmth of his presence sent a shiver tunneling down her spine. She tipped up her chin and met his wary gaze. "It's fine. You did exactly what needed to be done. Thank you."

Relief washed over his features. "You're welcome."

She tipped her head toward the barista. "We should get this to go so we can handle your family emergency."

"You'll get no argument from me."

A few minutes later, she carried their coffees

and a pastry box full of a dozen doughnuts out-side. Gus trailed her.

She stopped and turned. Pain etched his fea-tures. Poor guy. "You look like you're hurting."

"You're right. Pain's getting worse, and I need to see what Liesel wants."

"Maybe going out for coffee was a little too ambitious."

"Or maybe Jessica's a monster and pushed me too hard."

"Nice try. She's one of the best physical ther-apists we've ever had." Mia slowed her pace to match Gus's as they rounded the building and walked toward her car. "I'm sorry you're hurt-ing. I'll take you back to the house. Then you can call Liesel."

He eyed the box of doughnuts in her hand. "Who are those for?"

"These are part of my coping strategy. Dough-nuts make everything better."

"I like the way you think. Who is that lady, anyway?"

"Her husband used to be the mayor. She's a self-appointed mother hen. I'm sure her heart is in the right place, but more often than not, her nosiness stirs up trouble."

"Are you responsible for those details she mentioned?"

Mia sighed. "She was right. We do need to

secure chairs and tables from the equipment-rental place off the island."

"When's the commemoration?"

"May first."

"That's more than three months from now," Gus said. "Why is she so worried?"

"Mrs. Lovell's ability to sense when people aren't cooperating with her plans is incredible. It's almost like she knows I'm avoiding my assignment. Which doesn't do any good, because Lexi's going to come to Hearts Bay whether I'm ready to meet her or not. Stepping down from the committee changes nothing, and I feel guilty for shirking my responsibility, but there's something about volunteering that makes me want to leave the island. Permanently."

Oh, wow. She was a mess. Heat flushed her cheeks. "How's that for denial?"

"It's time to step down. Like I said yesterday, you don't owe anyone an explanation, either."

"But that's so selfish." She was almost thirty-five years old. A grown woman who handled medical emergencies for a living. Why couldn't she serve on a committee and attend a few meetings without having a meltdown?

Gus stopped walking and faced her. "It's not selfish to establish boundaries. Celebrating that event will bring Lexi here. Which will change your current circumstances forever. Your feelings are valid. Maybe not everyone here will understand where you're coming from, but that's on them."

"No, I'm not stepping down. I can do this."

His concerned gaze roamed her face. "Are you sure?"

She shook off the complicated emotions and kept walking. Maybe she'd been a little too honest. "Come on, let's get you back to my parents' place."

"How's your mom, by the way? I didn't see her this morning."

"She stayed overnight in the hospital. My dad and my sisters are taking turns sitting with her. We want to make sure we can bring her fever down." A chill raced through her. If Mom stayed trapped in this vicious cycle of fevers and frequent infections, they might have to transport her to Anchorage or back to Seattle until they identified a donor match.

"That's tough. I'm sorry."

"Thanks. We're all feeling discouraged." Yet another reason she needed to tell her whole family about Lexi. Sooner rather than later. Mom's condition kept deteriorating. If Lexi ended up being a viable donor, Mia would never forgive herself for stalling so long. Ugh. What a convoluted mess.

They arrived at her vehicle. She set the cof-

fee and doughnuts on the hood, then opened
the door for him.

"You don't have to do that. I can get in by
myself."

She tipped back her head and groaned at the
sky. So stubborn. "Let me help you, Gus."

He paused, his hand on the door, and shot
her look.

"I heard Jessica. She told you activities of
daily living are going to be tough for a while.
It's okay if I help you. It doesn't mean you're
weak."

He sank onto the edge of the seat, with one
leg inside the SUV and the other partway outside. She tried not to let her gaze linger on the
muscles evident beneath the cotton fabric of his
joggers. "So let me get this straight."

"I know what you're going to say. That I
don't want to hear advice, but I want you to
take mine."

His lips twitched with that impish smile.
Yeah, she wanted to see more of that. "Yes,
thank you for making my point."

"Our circumstances are not the same."

His blue eyes bore into her. Again with the
long look and the pointed silence. Oh, brother.
He was exasperating. "Do you want me to help
with your seat belt or not?"

He grinned. "Not."

"Fine." She waited for him to get settled, then gently closed the door, collected the pastries and the coffee and walked around to the driver's side. She didn't enjoy the trajectory of the conversation or the fact that she'd been so vulnerable with him, but she couldn't deny that she enjoyed being with Gus. The way his presence beside her made her feel protected. Seen.

Oh, brother. She rolled her eyes. She'd read one too many of her sister's romance novels lately. Because that kind of thinking would only get her in way too deep with a man she couldn't afford to fall in love with.

"I can't believe Carina didn't tell you she was going on bed rest. Who's going to watch her kids? What about Poppy? Isn't your mother still in New Mexico?"

Gus carefully shifted his weight and leaned against the headboard. He'd borrowed the Maddens' device again and retreated to his bedroom in the guesthouse to call Liesel. Somehow, he needed to convince her to bring Poppy to Hearts Bay. If only he could squeeze a word in. Her questions flew at him faster than he could process.

"My phone's somewhere at the bottom of the Gulf of Alaska, along with the vessel I was on. Not sure if you caught the part of the story where the *Imogene* sank. I'm blessed to be alive. Maybe Carina didn't want to bother me."

He wished Carina had told him she was going on bed rest, but there was nothing he could do to change the situation. Or be helpful. It bugged him that he had to hear the news from Liesel, though.

"It would be nice if your mother would come home. Especially now that you and Carina could use extra help." Even though the connection for the video call was glitchy, her expression made his scalp prickle. She wanted something. That flinty look in her eyes telegraphed her intentions.

"I'm sure Mom will come home once she's certain my grandfather has the care he needs. By the way, where's Poppy? Can I say hello?" He quickly scanned the familiar kitchen in the background, longing for a glimpse of his baby girl. Man, he missed her so much. Liesel had owned the house before they'd married. When they'd separated, he'd moved to a smaller rental close by. Dillingham had few options, but he'd made the new place feel like home.

"She's across the street, having a playdate with the neighbors."

Huh. Toddlers had playdates? Was he supposed to be arranging those when he had Poppy with him? He resisted the urge to ask. Liesel would only relish the opportunity to point out his shortcomings. No thank you.

"What's going on, Liesel?"

"I heard about your sister's high-risk pregnancy, Gus. Is it so wrong that I wanted to make sure you had a backup plan for childcare?"

Gus scrubbed his palm along his jaw. "I appreciate your concern, and I already have a plan."

He still didn't trust her. Her slender fingers fiddled with the locket at her neck. A sure sign that she was biding her time until she revealed her true motive for this conversation.

"So how long do you think you'll be in…" She trailed off, her smooth brow crinkling. "Where are you again?"

"Hearts Bay, Orca Island."

She grimaced. "You're a long way from home."

He swallowed back a frustrated groan. "Listen, I've got cracked ribs, a broken collarbone and a reinflated lung that's not exactly a picnic to live with. I just took my pain meds and I'm fading fast. Whatever you want from me let's cut to the chase, shall we?"

Something he couldn't quite decipher flickered in her eyes.

"All right." She sighed, then rolled her shoulders. "I need your help."

He couldn't stop a smile. "I'm sorry, what?"

She never admitted that she needed help. And certainly not from him. It probably almost killed her to even say those words.

"I know, I know." Liesel held up both palms toward the camera. "Please hear me out."

"I'm listening."

"I've accepted a special assignment with work. I'll be traveling frequently for the next three or four months visiting several villages, catching rides on the mail plane, checking in and letting residents in the communities know there's a female law-enforcement presence."

"Why?" He immediately regretted his flippant tone. "I mean, why you and why right now?"

"Because reports of domestic violence are on the rise. Winter is a challenging time, especially for the more remote villages. Most don't have officers on the payroll, so they rely on law enforcement from neighboring communities." Liesel gestured with her hands, her voice growing more passionate as she defended her professional commitments.

"Makes sense." He wanted to be supportive, or at least sound supportive. But all he could think of was how this affected Poppy.

"Our chief has been asked if we have anyone on staff that we can spare. I'm one of two female officers here, so I offered to take the assignment," Liesel said.

"What about Poppy?"

"That's why I wanted to speak with you."

He blew out a laugh, making his ribs scream at him. He tried shifting positions in the bed but nothing relieved the pain. "I might be in rough shape, but there's no way I'm letting you take our daughter with you in potentially dangerous conditions. We have an agreement, Liesel. A fifty-fifty co-parenting plan."

Something he'd fought hard for, because initially she hadn't wanted him to spend very much time with his daughter. Thankfully, mediation and a judge had implemented an arrangement they could all live with.

"Gus, I'd never even think of taking Poppy with me. My job is important, though. These villages need my help. You're not going to stay in Hearts Bay permanently, are you?"

His thoughts slid to Mia. A pleasant reminder that he wasn't alone. Whatever happened with this conversation, he'd have someone to rehash it with.

"Gus? Did you hear me?"

"I can't fly until I've recovered enough so the change in air pressure doesn't collapse my lung again."

"I thought that might be an issue." Liesel rubbed her hands together. "That's why I called your brother."

Her words slammed into him like a rogue crab pot on an ice-covered deck. His *brother*? The guy he hadn't spoken with in months? Maybe a year?

Liesel zipped the locket back and forth on the chain. "Unique problems call for creative solutions, right? Besides, I didn't think you'd be feeling well enough to come up with a plan. Let's face it, thinking ahead has never been your gift."

Ouch. He clutched part of his blanket in his fist. "You called my brother?"

"I called your sister first. Your brother evidently called her when he read a story online about your accident. See a pattern here? Your family cares about you, Gus. Even your brother."

Right. He hated that she had the power to poke all his chronic wounds. Including his frayed relationship with Dean. Darkness crept into his field of vision. A warm fuzzy sensation swept over him. Oh, how he wanted to sleep.

"I'm having trouble following the conversation." He fought to get the words out. Liesel's face on the screen appeared pixilated. The pain meds must be working. "Wh-what does my brother have to do with your job and Poppy?"

"Your brother said he's willing to do whatever he can to help. I…that he come and stay here…a few weeks—"

"Hold on." Gus struggled to stay alert. "Our connection is spotty. Did you say you're going to leave our daughter with an uncle she's never met? Are you sure that's wise?"

She winced. "Huh, that's ironic. He said the same thing. Well, what he actually said is 'I don't do kids,' but I think I have him convinced to do what I want him to."

Gus blew another breath through gritted teeth. "Is he still living in Montana?"

"I offered to split the cost of his ticket." She smiled triumphantly. "He's running out of viable excuses."

"You don't have to drag Dean into this, Liesel. I'm staying with some family friends of Abner's. They've already offered to let Poppy stay here, too. Why don't you bring her to me?"

Her smile vanished. She leaned in. "Are you even listening? I've asked your brother to help us because I need to leave as soon as possible. This isn't an opportunity I'm willing to pass up, Gus. I'll get hazard pay and it puts me in line for a promotion. The chief won't stay on here much longer. If all goes well, I'll be next in line for his job when he transfers."

"Isn't—isn't Poppy important to you?" He tipped back his head and let his eyelids fall closed. Liesel's explanation didn't add up. How long had she been planning to take on this special assignment? It didn't sound like a role that had opened overnight.

"Of course, she is. That's why I went to the trouble to call your brother."

"Tell the chief you're a single mom and I was injured. You—you can't help this time." The allure of sleep and relief from the pain made finding the right words a struggle. He just needed to rest. They could talk again tomorrow.

"Gus, open your eyes and listen to me. I've made plans for your brother to fly here, pick up Poppy and bring her to you."

Absolutely not.

He held up his hand to protest but flinched when the movement drove another spike of pain through his shoulder. Dumb move. And Liesel's big plan was quite possibly the dumbest idea she'd ever had. This would never work. Yes, he wanted his little girl here with him. It was the part about Dean that didn't sit well. Poppy would be terrified, traveling so far with his brother, a stranger to her.

"Gus? Are you there?"

He forced his eyes open. "Still here."

"Then it's all settled. I'll forward the email as soon as I have Dean and Poppy's flight info. Thanks for being flexible."

Gus tried to protest before Liesel ended the call, but couldn't wade through the thick sludge in his brain to form a sentence. As he drifted off, his thoughts returned to Mia. He imagined her beautiful eyes fixed on him, her capable hands treating his injuries. She'd been candid about her fears. Even though her parents had offered, he still hated that he had to impose on them by bringing Poppy and his brother into their lives. He owed them. Somehow, he'd convince Mia to help him initiate the stem-cell-donation process. It was the least he could do.

Chapter Five

Mia paced the floor between the sofa and re-cliner, wiped her sweaty palms on her jeans, then burrowed her hands in the pockets of her favorite cardigan sweater. A framed family photo on the bookshelf featuring her and her sisters standing on the deck of Charlie's boat caught her eye. The image stole her breath. She was about to tell her family that she likely wasn't a Madden. How was she supposed to find the words?

"Mia, we're ready to call Eliana." Tess stood in the kitchen's doorway with her newborn daughter, Lucy, strapped to her chest in a carrier. "Come in here and tell us your big news."

Mia's stomach churned. Rylee shot her an empathetic you've-got-this glance as Mia trudged into the kitchen. She joined her family around the large oval table. Her parents sat at one end.

Tess stood behind her husband, Asher, one hand on his shoulder as she swayed gently from side to side. Their son, Cameron, sat beside Asher, fidgeting with a silver-and-blue spinner.

Rylee carried a stack of empty plates and dishes from the table to the kitchen counter. They'd enjoyed a wonderful meal together. Despite her mother's recent stay in the hospital and her imminent need for a stem-cell transplant, her pink-tinged cheeks and sparkling eyes offered Mia hope.

Your announcement will wreck a peaceful evening.

The thought plunged her into another icy river of guilt. Maybe she should wait. Clutching the back of the empty chair until her knuckles turned white, she shifted her weight from one foot to the other. Asher tapped the button on the device and the familiar sound of a video call echoed from the speaker.

"Are you okay, sweetheart?" Her father's kind eyes found hers. "Why don't you sit down?"

"I'd rather stand." She forced out the words, suddenly wishing Gus was here. He'd excused himself a few minutes ago and made his way out to the guesthouse. She let her eyes travel to the chair he'd vacated. There was something about his presence. His quiet strength. Those eyes. Oh, those eyes. She gave herself a mental shake. Maybe it was better that he'd given her family privacy. He was proving to be quite the distraction.

Eliana appeared on the screen. She smiled and waved. "Hey, everyone. Happy New Year."

They'd chatted with her several times during the holidays. Eliana was in the last few weeks of a challenging pregnancy. She'd stayed in Idaho with her husband and the twins for Christmas. Hopefully, she'd be able to bring her new baby to Alaska in a few months.

"What's going on? What's the big news?" Eliana braced her chin in her hand and leaned close to the screen. "I can hardly stand the suspense."

Rylee squeezed past Mia, offering her a gentle pat on the shoulder before sliding into Gus's empty chair.

"Um, I…" Her heart thundered in her chest. She blew out a long breath then surveyed the expectant faces rimming the table. "I don't know how to say this exactly, so—"

"You've met someone!" Tess interrupted her, eyes gleaming. Her excitement provoked a muted cry from the tiny baby in the carrier.

"Tess." Their mother frowned then shook her head. "Let her speak."

Gus's face materialized in Mia's mind. She swallowed hard. "Well, I—"

"I knew it." Tess leaned down close to Asher. "Didn't I tell you she'd met someone?"

Asher smiled, then grabbed her hand and pressed a quick kiss to her knuckles. "You did."

Heat warmed Mia's skin and she stole a desperate glance at Rylee. Rylee grimaced then gestured for Mia to keep going.

"Did you meet him online?" Eliana asked. "Or is it someone local?"

"That visiting respiratory therapist who helped us today is a nice guy," Dad said. "Have you met him yet?"

Oh, boy. This was not going well. She pressed her fingertips to her forehead and massaged the ache forming there. She hadn't actually met anyone. Gus and Abner had been friends for years. But she couldn't let her thoughts keep wandering. This family meeting had nothing to do with Gus. Well, almost nothing.

Maybe she should wait. They were all going to be so shocked when she told them about Lexi. What if Lexi was right? What if this was really her family sitting here laughing, reminiscing, enjoying a good meal on a frigid winter night? What if Lexi had had a horrible upbringing? Meeting her biological family might be a fresh start she desperately needed.

"Mia." Rylee's voice pulled her back to reality. "Just tell us. No matter what you say, it's all going to work out. We love you."

Tears pricked the backs of Mia's eyes. "Okay, here goes. A woman named Lexi Thomas from Georgia contacted me via social media before Christmas. I was stunned when I got her message because..."

Her heart crawled up into her throat. Oh, she couldn't do this. She did not want to be the one to tell her family—not because she didn't want them to know, but because she wasn't prepared for what they might say. How they would respond.

"She says that she and I were switched at birth after the volcanic eruption. She claims to have proof and wants to come here and meet all of you because she believes that you are her family."

"No. Way." Eliana's declaration was the only sound in the room. She clamped her hands over her mouth. Even Cameron sat still, his eyes roaming the faces around the table.

Dad cleared his throat. Reached for his wife's hand. Mom's chin wobbled and her face turned pale.

"Mom, Dad, please say something," Mia whispered.

"Honey, I think you should sit down," Dad said.

Tess and Mia exchanged glances. Her legs felt

like limp spaghetti noodles as she pulled out the chair and sank into it. "You all are acting like maybe this isn't a surprise," she said, barely able to choke out the words. She wrapped her arms around her torso and a hollow ache filled her stomach. This was what she'd worried about. That they had known and hadn't told her.

"Stories of babies being switched that day have circulated the island over the years." Mom dabbed at the corners of her eyes with a tissue. "A few folks made comments here and there about your hair color. Things of that nature, but, sweetheart, that was such a chaotic day. Eight babies were born within a few hours of each other."

"A volcano had erupted. We couldn't evacuate the island, so they ordered us to shelter in place." Her father's eyes filled with empathy. "Everyone did the best they could in a horrible situation."

"So you didn't know that I wasn't your baby?"

"There's no way I could've known," Mom said. "They placed a baby in my arms. I was told it was the girl I had delivered. They'd managed to get the ID bands on us and ours matched. You didn't have any hair yet, and you looked like a newborn. Honestly, to me you didn't look that much different from Charlie."

"What about you, Dad? What did you think?"

Her father offered her a tender smile. "Mia, you are our daughter. You always have been. You always will be. You are a wonderful sister and a loyal friend. A fantastic PA. You matter. If we took everything that people said on this island as the truth, we'd be in a world of hurt."

"People love to tell stories," Tess whispered.

"Especially the juicy, scandalous ones." Asher glanced up at his wife. Tess planted a quick kiss on his lips.

Mia averted her gaze. They were bugging her. Couldn't they hold off on the public displays of affection for more than three minutes? "If Lexi and I were switched at birth, you're saying you wouldn't be entirely shocked?"

Her parents looked at each other, then Mom lifted one shoulder. "That day was both horrific and amazing all at the same time. We survived a natural disaster and welcomed our second child into the world. It's entirely possible, during the chaos, that someone made a mistake. But there was no reason for us to believe that you'd been switched with another baby."

"Then what am I supposed to tell Lexi?" Mia asked.

Her family all started talking at once. They speculated what it must be like for the young woman to want to come to Alaska all the way from Georgia. How excited she was to meet her family. They wondered what she looked like. If she had any siblings. The conversation continued, and the longer they chatted, the more everyone came up with new questions, rather than answers.

Mia blinked back tears. She'd never felt more forgotten or alone. When her phone buzzed, she quickly pounced on it.

All eyes shifted her way, as if they suddenly remembered she was there. "Is that her? Did she know you were going to talk to us tonight?" Tess asked.

A simple message from Lexi appeared on the screen.

Have you spoken with your family yet?

She put the phone back down on her lap without responding. "I didn't tell her I was going to talk to you tonight, but I promised that I would get back to her soon. She wants to make plans to visit."

"Oh, my." Her mother pressed her fingers to her lips.

"Wait." Mia held up one finger. "We can't talk about Lexi without talking about your need for a viable donor. If she is your daughter, that means you now have another potential match."

"Oh, dear," Tess said. "I hadn't thought about that."

I have. Mia resisted the urge to be catty or gloat. "It's not really my place to tell her your private medical information, but I'm also not going to pretend that I haven't wondered if she solves your problem."

Mom leaned her head against Dad's shoulder. He pressed his cheek to the top of her head then closed his eyes.

"Can I go play a game on your phone, Dad?" Cameron shoved back his chair. "This isn't fun."

He wasn't wrong. She tried not to be annoyed. They had yet to ask her how she felt about all this. What this news meant for her. She stood quietly and cleared more plates from the table, hoping her family would notice, but they didn't.

"Aunt Mia, check this out," Cameron called over his shoulder as he zipped into the living room. She'd never been so thankful for her nephew in her life. She followed him into the living room and sat down on the sofa. He squeezed in next to her, his dad's phone in hand. He showed her a game with creatures and jewels on the screen. She tried to listen to his detailed explanation, but struggled to focus.

The back door opened, then shut. The sound of Gus's careful footsteps approaching, followed by the familiar aroma of his cologne, teased her senses. Butterflies danced in her stomach as she sensed him standing behind the sofa.

Cameron twisted around and looked at him. "Hey, Mr. Gus, what's up?"

"I heard there was dessert. Do you know anything about that?"

Cameron shot off the sofa, dropped the phone on the coffee table and ran back into the kitchen. "Mom, Dad, are we having dessert?"

"That was easy." Gus sat down beside her on the sofa. His eyes locked on hers. "How are you doing?"

Her eyes dipped to his broad chest. She wondered what it would feel like to lean against him and cry into the fabric of his soft cotton shirt.

"Mia?"

"I told them. I can't really say for sure how it went. They have a lot of questions."

"You don't have to find all the answers."

Oh, but I do.

How else would they find out how she and Lexi had been switched if she didn't keep searching for more information? Pressing her lips together, she battled back the emotion that had lodged like a boulder in her throat. The warmth of his hand gently clasping her shoulder made her breath hitch.

"This is awful," she whispered.

"You're going to get through this. They are still your family, and they love you. Whether you're connected by the same gene pool or not."

She stared at the flames crackling in the fireplace, desperate for small comfort in the details she'd always associated with family. With home. She wanted to believe him. But already, she felt alone and forgotten. They seemed much more interested in hearing about Lexi than how this news had turned her world upside down.

The sudden longing to pull her close and kiss away her heartache scared him. That couldn't happen. He inched away, deliberately draping his arm across the back of the sofa. He leaned hard into the cushions. His mind scrambled for something benign to ponder. Pounds of crab in the targeted quota. How many miles equaled a nautical mile. His high-school locker combo. Anything. Anything at all that might occupy his thoughts and douse the itch in his fingers to smooth back her hair.

Stop.

He didn't know her well enough to be her source of comfort. After all she'd done for him, he had no right to offer anything but gratitude. But even in the short time they'd spent together, plus the few times they'd interacted when Abner was alive, he could see that she was hurting.

"Did your parents say whether they knew someone might've mixed up the babies?" Man, he didn't even know how to frame this conversation appropriately. What were you supposed to say to someone who was facing the very difficult realization that their biological family wasn't their own?

Almost everyone in south-central Alaska had been affected by that volcanic eruption. Older generations rarely wanted to talk about the horror they'd witnessed, but occasionally they shared parts of their story with younger family members. Another eruption or a tsunami from seismic activity was always a possibility. Gus hadn't encountered anyone who lived in fear of another natural disaster destroying their communities, though. They all knew the evacuation routes and ran through the drills. Kept their homes and businesses up to code. Here on Orca Island, the threat seemed more critical because they didn't really have an evacuation route. These folks lived differently because of their isolated lifestyle.

"They're aware of rumors that babies might've been switched." Mia glanced over her shoulder toward the kitchen. "Evidently my parents never felt the need to follow up and see if I was involved. They don't seem to have any additional details."

Gus surveyed her features. Her mouth was drawn tight. The place between her eyebrows was etched with confusion. He folded his hand into a fist to keep from drawing her into an embrace. Part of him wanted to stand up and defend her. Point out to the people gathered around the table that their reaction to Mia's news had hurt her.

Knives and forks clinked against plates. The hum of pleasant conversation filtered through the air. They weren't behaving like a family dealing with a scandal.

"What's wrong?" Mia shifted toward him. Her green eyes scanned his face, then toggled to his arm and shoulders, then back to his face. "Are you in pain?"

"Not really." He wasn't ever not in pain these days, but the throbbing in his arm and chest wasn't the white-hot fire he'd endured in the hospital. "I'll be fine. I'm worried about you, though. What are you going to do now?"

"I promised Lexi I would get back to her soon. She deserves to know that I've shared her news with my—our—family. I guess that means I should make arrangements to meet her—my—parents."

"That's a big step," Gus said. "Do you think you're ready for that?"

Mia looked away. "I don't think I'll ever be ready."

Her hair spilled forward, a coppery red curtain reflecting the light from the lamp on the end table. He reached out to rub her back, then quickly pulled away. Gripping the back of the sofa tighter, he forced himself to remain still. Abner might be dead and gone, but that didn't mean Gus had the right to feel anything other than friendship toward Mia. She was wading through the biggest crisis of her life. On top of trying to help her mother find a donor match. Her family had helped him in his darkest hour. The last thing he needed to do was introduce a romantic relationship into this complicated equation.

"Will you please explain the process for stem-cell donation again?"

Mia sat back on the sofa. "The initial step is easy. A cheek swab then some lab work. Why? Do you think I should ask Lexi to get tested?"

"That's probably a good idea, but it wasn't Lexi that I was thinking of."

Her eyes widened. "Gus, we've talked about this already. You could have died in that accident. Now you're offering to take part in a stem-cell transplant?"

"Is there something wrong with my offer? Why are you being so skeptical?"

"I'm not." She fiddled with a button on her sweater. "Okay, so yeah, maybe I am a little skeptical. But you keep telling me how much you need to see your daughter and that you're planning to go back to work. If you're a viable match for someone who needs a transplant, they'll want you to move quickly. Donating is at least a week-long commitment. Not to mention you'll have to travel to Anchorage. I don't think you realize what you're offering."

He wouldn't let her doubt squash his enthusiasm. "I understand and I still want to help. Since going back to Dillingham isn't an option right now, my brother, Dean, has offered to bring Poppy here. He's planning to arrive on the afternoon flight tomorrow."

Her mouth opened then closed, then opened again. She reached over and gently clasped his forearm. "Gus, that's amazing. Why didn't you say something?"

The warmth of her touch sent a familiar wave of attraction zipping through his extremities.

"I only found out two days ago, and I didn't want to say anything until I knew for sure Dean and Poppy had flights booked. I realize this is a huge imposition. The last thing I want to do is take advantage of your kindness. We'll bunk in the guesthouse and try our best to stay out of your way."

She smiled. "It's not a problem. Your brother and Poppy are more than welcome here."

"As a thank-you for your generosity, I want to start the screening process for being a donor.

Surely there's a place on the island where I can get my cheek swabbed?"

"There is." Mia blew out a long breath. He hated that she was stressed. And that her family hadn't paid any attention to her emotional needs right now. His eyes traced the path of her hand as it dropped into her lap. Again, he wrestled with the temptation to reach for her, twine his fingers through hers and promise that they'd find a way forward. Together.

Whoa. You are out of control.

He slammed the door on the notion. There was no way he could act on his feelings.

Chapter Six

"Dude, I thought that pilot was never going to land that plane." Dean Coleman huffed out an exasperated breath as he set Poppy's car seat on the industrial gray carpet. Her pink-and-yellow backpack and his own black duffel bag both slid from his shoulders and landed at his feet.

"Da-da!" Poppy shouted, squirming in Dean's arms.

Man, she was adorable. Gus sank gingerly to one knee in the middle of Hearts Bay's tiny airport. Ignoring Dean's commentary about the rough flight, Gus focused all his attention on Poppy. A fractured collarbone and a stupid chest tube wouldn't keep him from embracing his baby girl.

The other passengers entering the airport from their flight sidestepped the Coleman mini reunion, tossing them amused glances as they passed.

"Hang on." Dean awkwardly set Poppy on her feet.

As soon as her sneakers touched the floor, she toddled toward Gus with her little arms outstretched.

"Poppy." He pulled her to him, gritting his teeth through the familiar pain as he closed his eyes. "I've missed you so much."

She sagged against his chest and buried her face in his flannel button-down. Her little body trembled. Poor thing. They'd expected too much of her, making her leave home then take two flights with an uncle she didn't know.

Gus breathed in the faint aroma of her baby shampoo, then pressed a tender kiss to the top of her soft blond hair. He slowly pulled back, scanning her from head to toe.

She flashed a toothy grin. Tears still clung to her eyelashes and her pale skin was blotchy.

"We've had a couple of spills." Dean brushed at a mysterious stain on the sleeve of his gray hooded sweatshirt. "Do you think Liesel packed extra clothes in her bag?"

Gus tried to push to his feet, but she clutched the sleeve of his shirt.

"It's okay, sweet pea. Daddy's here. Let me stand up and say hello to Uncle Dean."

Poppy tapped his sling. "Ouchy?"

"Yeah, I've got a few ouchies right now. Don't

worry. I'm getting better." He grunted then stood and extended his hand toward his younger brother. "Hey, man. It's good to see you."

"You, too." Dean's haggard features morphed into a thin smile. "You've got a cute kid there."

Gus let go of Dean's hand and pulled Poppy close again. "Thank you. I hope the trip wasn't too rough."

Dean's smile faded and he shook his head. "I don't know why I let Liesel talk me into this."

Gus let that comment go. It didn't matter who'd convinced Dean to make the trip. He was here. With Poppy in tow.

"Why don't we get the bags and then catch up later." Dean slung Poppy's backpack over his shoulder then grabbed his black duffel bag with his other hand.

From the corner of his eye, Gus spotted Mia hovering. Waiting patiently. Poppy leaned against his leg. She'd already wedged her thumb in her mouth. Her wide-eyed gaze bounced back and forth between them.

"I'm glad you both made it here safely," Gus said. "Come on, baggage claim is this way."

They turned toward the carousels at the opposite end of the building. "I'd like you to meet a friend of mine. Mia, this is my brother, Dean, and my daughter, Poppy," Gus said.

Mia's beautiful smile instantly thawed the

tension hovering between Gus and his brother. How had they gone more than a year without any meaningful conversation? Another wave of guilt sluiced through his veins, reminding him of all the ways he'd failed the people he cared about.

"It's nice to meet you, Mia." Dean offered his hand. "How do you and Gus know each other?"

"It's nice to meet you, too." Her smile faltered.

Gus didn't want to explain their connection. "Mia and I have mutual friends."

"I see." Dean shot him a knowing look. "Small world and all, right?"

"Something like that." Gus glanced down at Poppy. She pulled her thumb from her mouth and reached for his hand. He didn't mind that her fingers were still soggy. It was hard to believe she was here. As much as Liesel infuriated him, he had to admit he was grateful that her plans had come together.

"Did you like riding in an airplane?" he asked her.

She scrunched her little nose. "Yuck."

They followed the rest of the passengers toward the baggage-claim area. Poppy pointed at the mural painted on the wall featuring the island's most popular animals.

Gus slowed down and named a few for her. "That's a brown bear, a black-tailed deer and a bald eagle."

She quickly lost interest, distracted by the bright lights on a nearby vending machine.

"This way, kiddo." Gus redirected her to the baggage claim.

Mia stood between him and Dean beside the silver carousel. "Gus said you live in Montana?"

"For now." Dean deposited both carry-ons next to his battered work boots.

"And what do you do?"

Dean yawned, then scrubbed his palm over his face. "Coach wrestling, work for a guy who runs a sporting-goods store, sometimes I deliver pizza. In the summer, I work as a guide for people who want to do tours in the national park."

"Wow, sounds exciting," Mia said.

"Pays the bills."

The conveyor belt jerked to a start with a buzz that captured Poppy's attention. An orange caution light flashed on the wall nearby.

Dean gestured at a suitcase sliding toward them. "That's mine."

He stepped away to collect the bag. Mia shifted her attention to Poppy. "Your daughter is precious."

"Thank you." He gently squeezed Poppy's hand. "Can you say hello to Mia?"

Poppy stared up at Mia, then wedged her thumb back in her mouth.

Anxiety crawled across his skin. Mia, who

he'd always regarded as his best friend's girlfriend, was quickly becoming so much more than that. Yeah, okay, so she'd rescued him and treated his injuries. But she was becoming someone he deeply cared about. Now she was meeting his daughter for the first time.

What if this didn't go well? What if Mia didn't even like kids?

That hardly seemed possible. She was a natural with her nephew, Cameron. They should've talked about this. They should've talked about so many things before he let their worlds collide on this island.

How adorable was this little girl?

Mia dropped to her knees beside the baggage carousel. Poppy's blond hair matched her father's. She also had Gus's startling blue eyes. She had on a puffy turquoise-blue jacket, jeans with snowflakes embroidered on the flared legs and the most adorable pink sneakers Mia had ever seen.

Gus glanced down at her. Uncertainty flickered in his eyes. "Are you all right?"

"Yeah, I'm great. Why? I thought I'd keep Poppy entertained so you guys could, you know…" She gestured with her hand back and forth between Gus and Dean. "Catch up."

"Right." Gus nodded. He stayed rooted in place.

"Poppy, which bag is yours?" Mia pointed at the small train of duffel bags and suitcases inching toward them on the carousel. Poppy glanced up at Gus again, her expression serious.

She clearly adored her father, with her tiny little fingers wound around his strong hand. Mia's phone hummed in her pocket. She plucked it out and glanced at the screen.

Lexi.

Her stomach tightened. They'd played phone tag all week. Between the time difference, Mia's work schedule and Lexi juggling her commitments, they'd struggled to connect. She hesitated, then dropped the phone back in her jacket pocket. Selfish? Probably. She'd brought Gus here to pick up his daughter and brother. This wasn't the time to have this conversation with Lexi. Not in the middle of the airport.

"Mia, what do you do for work?" Dean set his suitcase next to Poppy's backpack.

Where Gus was tall and broad and filled the room with his presence, his younger brother was compact. Stocky. Probably not any less strong, though. He was wearing Carhartt brown pants and a hoodie advertising a university in Montana.

"I'm a physician assistant here on the island."

"Oh, right on." Dean cut his blue eyes toward Gus. "Were you on shift when he was in the hospital?"

"I was." She stole a quick glance at Gus. They hadn't spoken in depth about his family. She mentally scrolled through her memories of past conversations with Abner. He hadn't shared much about Gus's family life, either. What little she had heard hinted at heartache. Tension hovered over Gus and Dean like an angry storm cloud.

"It's nice what you're doing, helping Gus and Poppy out. Hopefully he'll be able to travel before too long." She offered Gus what she hoped was an encouraging smile. The pained expression on his face made her wish she could pluck the words right back. Maybe she was causing problems with her meaningless small talk.

"Look." Poppy jumped up and down and pointed. A smattering of laughter flowed from the men and women waiting nearby for their bags.

"Is that yours?" Mia asked.

Poppy ran toward the carousel, but a dog barking from a crate nearby startled her. She squealed then ran back to Gus, clutching at his arm again.

He grimaced. No doubt Poppy's tugging and pulling didn't bode well for his healing injuries.

"Here." Mia stepped closer to Poppy. "May I

hold your hand or help you get your bag? Your daddy's body is still kind of sore."

As Poppy studied her, then reluctantly took Mia's outstretched hand, all her concerns vanished. Friendship meant helping one another. She could hang out with Poppy and not get too attached.

"Thanks for doing this." Gus had claimed the recliner in the Maddens' guesthouse. The trip to the airport and keeping Poppy occupied had drained the last of his meager energy reserves.

"No problem." Dean had sprawled on the floor beside the brown leather sofa and the wood-burning fireplace. "This is by far the nicest guesthouse I've ever stayed in."

"They built it for a grandmother who doesn't want to move in." Gus surveyed their surroundings. A beautiful live-edge slab of cedar on a basic pedestal served as a coffee table. A flat-screen TV was mounted on the opposite wall, and framed photos of Alaskan wildlife, gorgeous sunsets and a fishing boat dotted the remaining walls. The fully functional kitchen and bathroom supplied everything he'd needed. He still couldn't get over the Madden family's incredible generosity. Mia had dismissed his offer to help Mrs. Madden find a donor match. But really, it was the only way he could think of to adequately repay them.

"What dis?" Poppy held up a rubber yellow duck and small book with vinyl pages. There were only two bedrooms in the house, which she'd thoroughly explored already. She'd spent the last few minutes meandering between Dean, Gus and a plastic bin full of toys they'd borrowed from one of Mia's sisters.

"I'm happy to help." Dean accepted the book Poppy handed him and pretended to read it. She plopped down on the floor beside him and leaned closer, jabbering and pointing at the brightly colored illustrations.

"You flew from Montana to Dillingham, picked up a kid you'd never met, then flew two more flights to bring her here." Gus sucked in a breath as a sharp pain pierced his shoulder. "I'd say you went above and beyond the call of brotherly duty."

Dean turned the page in Poppy's book but didn't say anything.

Gus grew still. Had he aggravated him? He hadn't meant to sound ungrateful. "Dean, I'm serious. I really appreciate this. Liesel and I struggle to get along. Keeping Poppy safe is a priority. But we don't always agree on what's best."

He clamped his mouth shut. Oh, man. Now he was blabbering on about his issues with his ex.

Dean nodded. "I get that."

"You do?"

"Believe it or not, I didn't come back to Alaska just to help you."

"Oh." Gus picked up the ball he'd tucked between his leg and the side of the chair. He was supposed to be squeezing the dumb thing a gazillion times a day as part of his home-exercise program. "Are you here for a job interview?"

Dean pushed to a seated position. Poppy took that as an invitation to plunk down on his lap. She looked up at him, clearly ready for him to read to her.

Gus chuckled. "She wants you to read that book."

"There aren't any words." Dean frowned. "Just pictures."

"Yeah, I know. Make something up."

Dean shook his head. "Poppy, I don't want to read right now. Let's do something else."

Her little brow puckered. She eyed the ball in Gus's hand. "Ball?"

"Go look in the toy box." Gus pointed toward the container on the floor. "This one's for me. Go see if you can find one for you."

She climbed from her uncle's lap and returned to the bin. Then she dumped the whole thing out until a squishy purple ball rolled across the carpet.

"There you go," Gus said. "That one's yours."

"Yeah, we probably won't do much damage with that." Dean held out his hands. "Roll it to me."

Poppy sank to her knees and shoved the ball toward Dean. He caught it then gently rolled it back. She giggled then pounced on it.

"So if you're not here to rescue your wounded, single-dad brother, and you don't have a job interview lined up, then why are you here?"

"I want to visit Dad."

Dean's words gutted him. Never in a million years did he expect that to be his response.

"At the prison in Seward?" Gus barely squeezed the words out.

Dean nodded.

Gus released a low whistle. "Wow. You're a better man than I am."

"Listen, I know what he did to Carina was not okay, and—"

"And what he did to you was not okay, either."

Dean paused, then he drew a breath and continued. "I have had years of therapy to work through that. I'm in a better place now."

Gus cleared the emotion wedged in his throat. "But you both took the brunt of his rage."

The horror of those moments in their family's home, especially the final time Dean had stood up for them, crept in. Dad's rage. Gus's desperate longing for a safe place to hide. To avoid harm. The frightening anger that had bubbled up, propelling Dean toward their father until—

He squeezed his eyes shut, determined to block out the memories. His extremities tingled with the urge to run. Not that he could. But he'd rather be anywhere than right here.

They couldn't talk about this. Not now. "Dean, that's all in the past."

Dean rubbed his fingers slowly along his jaw.

Gus squeezed the ball in his hand as hard as he could, bracing for a confrontation.

"That doesn't mean we don't need to talk about what happened." Dean caught the ball Poppy rolled to him then rolled it back. "We're adults now. Isn't there anything you want to say?"

"Nope."

"Really?" Dean scraped his hand over his face. "Our dad's in prison for the rest of his life."

"Good."

"He won't get to know his grandkids. Does he even know about Poppy?"

"Probably not."

"Have you been to see him?"

Anger simmered in his gut. "I can't."

"I respect your decision," Dean said quietly. "It's important to me that I visit him."

"And say what exactly?"

"I'll figure that out when I get there."

Gus dug his fingers into the ball, resisting the urge to throw it across the room. *Help me to stay calm, Lord. Please. I can't come unglued in front of Poppy.*

The desperate prayer helped him take his outrage down a notch. That and Poppy's adorable squeal as her simple game with Dean continued. Her excitement softened the frayed rope of his frazzled emotions.

"I can't shake the need to see him. The guy shouldn't live the rest of his life with zero contact from his family," Dean said.

"If that's what you want to do while you're in Alaska, he'd probably appreciate the visit. I'm just... I'm not there yet. I wish I was, but I'm not." Gus set the ball on the side table and reached for the yellow rubber resistance band to continue his exercises.

"No judgment here." Dean offered Poppy a set of stackable plastic cups. "We endured things no child ever should."

Gus scooted forward and anchored the rubber band under his foot, avoiding Dean's gaze. "Thank you."

"For what?"

"For taking the brunt of his anger."

"Carina endured far worse."

"But you stepped up and intervened when no

one else would. Or could. I've always admired you for that," Gus said.

Dean's expression pinched. "I shouldn't have waited so long. I—"

Gus held up his palm to interrupt, his set of ten bicep curls only halfway completed. "You saved her life, Dean. All of our lives, really."

Dean shook his head in disbelief.

Gus let the conversation drop. What else was he supposed to say? He hadn't expected to see his brother, much less take a deep dive into Coleman family drama. He'd tried so hard to put the past behind him. But somehow, it always came slinking back in. Their father's abuse—not only the unspeakable acts that had harmed their sister, but also his frighteningly erratic behavior—had left wounds Gus feared would never heal.

Sure, he'd been to counseling. Plenty of it. And he prayed, but his fledgling faith left him with a mountain of doubt and so many questions. How could a good God who loved and cared about His children not have done anything to stop a man from harming his own innocent kids?

Poppy's ball rolled under the sofa. She fussed, then took the cups from Dean, squealing as she smacked two together.

Dean leaned back on his hands, a smile tugging at one side of his mouth. "What's going on with you and the lady who picked us up at the airport?"

Warmth crawled up Gus's neck at the mention of Mia. "Nothing."

"She's single, then?"

Gus fixed Dean with his most frigid stare. "Why, are you interested?"

Well. That came out a little sharper than he'd intended.

"Easy." Dean held up his palm. "Not for me, man. I've got somebody special back in Montana."

"Good."

He had a few exercises he was supposed to do to increase his range of motion. Not that he had any hope of dodging Dean's questions now. At least if he faced the wall, he didn't have to look Dean in the eye and risk giving away his true feelings for Mia.

"She seems nice," Dean said.

Gus winced against the discomfort as he gently walked his fingertips up the wall beside the door. "She was engaged to Abner Rossi. I was supposed to be the best man in their wedding."

"Oh. I didn't realize that was her."

Poppy's footsteps padded across the room then she slammed into the back of his legs, knocking him off balance. Without thinking,

Gus pressed both arms against the wall. Pain radiated through his arms, shoulders and across chest. He bit back a groan to keep from scaring her.

"Uh-oh." Dean hurried over. "You okay, dude?"

Gus nodded, but the pain made him queasy. He turned and patted his little girl on the head. "Why don't you find another game to play with Uncle Dean?"

"Come on, Poppy." Dean motioned for her to follow him to the toy box. "Let's see what else we have here."

Gus made his way back to the recliner. "The thing is, I still feel guilty for not being on board the boat when Abner and Charlie drowned."

Dean turned and pinned him with a long look. "Because you could've saved them?"

Gus swallowed hard against the tightness in his throat and sank into the chair. He couldn't speak. Man, he hadn't planned on going there, either.

"Gus, you're here for a reason. You have Poppy and a whole future ahead of you. I doubt Mia holds you solely responsible for the loss of her fiancé and her brother."

"Maybe not solely responsible." Gus reached for his sling. "But she knows I didn't show up for work that day."

"She can't hold a grudge forever. I mean, it's been a few years."

"It's been almost four years. Not that it matters. She's just doing her job. Her kindness toward me has nothing to do with a romantic relationship."

"That's why you're staying in her guesthouse and she's driving you all over town, helping you put your life back together."

"She's the one that grounded me until my lung fully recovers." Gus gingerly slipped his arm back into the sling.

Dean helped Poppy open a box of plastic magnetic tiles. "If Mia insists leaving the island will negatively impact your health, then use her orders for your good. With your charm and good looks, it shouldn't take long to win her over."

"Ha. I appreciate the pep talk. But Mia and I are not meant to be."

At least that's what he kept telling himself.

Chapter Seven

"Whoa. That's a lot of little kids." Mia surveyed the multipurpose room that was teeming with at least a dozen children under the age of three. Maybe the most toddlers she'd seen in one room since she'd done her pediatric rotation in PA school.

When Tess told her about the weekly playdate for babies and toddlers at the local community center, Mia had shared the info with Gus, thinking he'd decline. But he'd been more than happy to go. Now, Gus was standing nearby, kicking a pink tie-dye-colored rubber ball across the padded blue mat toward Poppy. Every time she stopped the ball, she shrieked and then flung it back at him.

He had an appointment tomorrow with Dr. Baldwin at the clinic. She fully expected the doctor would evaluate Gus then extract his chest tube. The next step toward him healing and being able to leave the island. Soon. But did she want him to go back to Dillingham? Her feelings were a tangled mess when it came to Gus.

Tess sat beside Mia on some folding chairs lined up against the wall. She was holding Lucy in her arms.

"How are things going?" Tess adjusted the pink-and-white polka-dot blanket she'd swaddled around her daughter. "I heard Gus's brother brought the little girl to the island?"

"Yesterday. His name's Dean."

"Where is he right now?"

"Probably sleeping in. Gus wanted to give him the morning off. That's part of the reason we agreed to meet you here."

"We?" Tess grinned. "I like the sound of that."

"Stop." Mia gently nudged her in the shoulder. "Gus and I are just…"

"Yeah, yeah. You're 'just friends.' That's what people who are interested in each other always say."

"Because it's true. We are friends. I helped him. He and Abner were very close. It wasn't like I could turn my back on him. He showed up in the emergency room in the middle of the night with a collapsed lung and—"

"All right. All right. I don't need all the details." Tess grimaced then carefully shifted Lucy to the crook of her other arm. "He keeps looking over here at you, and you keep looking over at him. Maybe it's my postpartum hormones, making me think irrational thoughts, but you guys kind of act like you're into each other."

"We're not."

"There's not even a possibility?"

"No," Mia snapped. Oh, that came out way too forceful.

"I didn't mean to upset you. I'm sorry." Tess gently squeezed her arm. "If you truly want to remain single, then I'll back off."

"I know you mean well, Tess." Mia shifted in her chair. "I'm just not sure marriage and motherhood are what God has planned for me. I'm turning thirty-five this year."

She let her gaze wander back to Poppy. The little girl looked adorable in her hot pink sweatpants and matching hot pink hoodie. She'd abandoned her shoes and socks already. She scooped up the ball and ran toward Gus. He gently kneeled and hugged her with one arm, then planted a quick kiss on top of her head. She stared up at him with a look that could only be described as pure adoration.

Attraction bloomed like a field of forget-me-nots on a summer day. Her feelings for him were changing. He was no longer just Abner's injured friend who had survived a horrible accident. Despite her doubts and fears about becoming attached to a guy with a questionable reputation, Gus had already become more than just someone staying at her parents' guesthouse while his injuries healed.

What in the world was she supposed to do with these feelings? He had Poppy to think about. And it wasn't like he was going stop being a crab fisherman. He had been sidelined because he couldn't use his arms. After losing Charlie and Abner, she'd promised herself she'd never fall for another fisherman. Even if she wanted to be a wife and a mother, Gus could never be anything more than a good friend.

Could he?

"No one will think less of you if you start dating again," Tess said. "You don't have to stay single as some sort of…tribute to Abner. He'd want you to be happy."

"I know. It's all so…complicated."

Tess stood. "Would you mind holding her? I need to run to the restroom."

Without waiting for Mia to object, Tess pressed Lucy into Mia's arms. Mia accepted the swaddled newborn. *Oh, my.* She hadn't been prepared for the way holding Lucy made her feel. Her insides had turned all warm and gooey, and yet she felt a fierce need to protect this helpless infant. She stared down at the sleeping baby, with her perfect skin and tiny nose and long eyelashes. Tess had dressed Lucy in the cutest gray striped pair of pajamas with a pink-and-gray elephant pattern. Mia was afraid to move. Afraid to disturb her. She'd held Lucy shortly after she'd been born, but the experience hadn't been this intense. Today, the overwhelming need to have a baby of her own nearly flattened her.

Where was this coming from?

"How old is the baby?" Gus lowered himself into the chair beside her.

"She's about six weeks now."

"You look good holding her."

Gus's compliment washed over her. She couldn't tear her eyes away from Lucy's flawless features, though. "Thanks, I guess. I don't get to hold many babies these days. Only when I handle pediatric appointments. Those don't allow for much time to snuggle the little ones. The parents kind of frown upon that."

Oh, boy. She was babbling. Again.

Gus's laugh rumbled in his chest, provoking a much different kind of feeling on the inside. She loved his laugh. Add that to his list of characteristics that were becoming nearly impossible to ignore.

He leaned back, stretched out his long legs and crossed one ankle over the other. Dean must've brought him some clothes because he looked much more at ease in his own worn jeans with a plaid button-down layered over a dark T-shirt. Poppy had found another child about her age and size to play with. They were stacking wooden blocks and knocking them down.

"Thanks for telling me about this. Dean needed time to himself and it's good for Poppy to get out and see some other kids her age."

"Do you get a lot of playdates back home?"

"I don't. Single dad hanging out with other moms and their kids isn't really my scene."

"It's what you're doing right now."

His gaze swung to meet hers. The emotions swimming in those fathomless pools of blue made her breath hitch. "This is different."

"How so?"

"Because you're here."

"Ah." She couldn't stop a smile. "I'm flattered."

His gaze held hers. "You should be."

Her mouth went dry. All she could do was grin like an idiot. Wow, she was terrible at flirting.

Gus averted his gaze. Finally. "Hopefully this will exhaust Poppy and she'll take a long nap this afternoon. I'm sure she's overwhelmed. This has been a lot of change for a toddler."

"It's been a lot for everybody. How are you holding up?"

"I'm all right." Gus ran his fingers over his short hair and smoothed it down. "I'm getting restless, to be honest. It still hasn't quite sunk in that the boat's gone and I don't have a job. Now my brother, whom I've barely spoken to in a long time, is here. Poppy's here. It's a lot to handle at once."

Lucy stirred in her arms. Mia carefully shifted in her chair, hoping their conversation didn't wake her. "Poppy sure is cute."

The little girl beside Poppy knocked over their tower of blocks. Mia braced for a tantrum. Instead, Poppy clapped her hands, then tipped back her head and laughed.

Gus chuckled again, the sound low and soft and even more appealing than the last time. "Yeah, she's a lot of fun." He glanced down at Lucy. "The newborn stage is so challenging. They're helpless, you know? I feel a little more confident now that Poppy can communicate some."

"And get into everything? Make messes?"

"She's certainly curious." His piercing gaze found hers again as his smile faded. "How about you? Have you ever thought about having kids?"

Her stomach plummeted and she quickly looked away. It was one thing to wrestle with the notion internally, and quite another to discuss it with a handsome single dad. "I don't know. Work keeps me busy. It would be hard to step away from that and focus on raising a family."

"Health-care workers have children, too, you know," he said, keeping his tone light. Teasing.

"All this new information about my parents not being who I thought they were and finding out that I have this whole mysterious other family out there somewhere makes me question everything."

After Abner died, she'd pushed aside her dreams of motherhood. That part wasn't something she cared to admit to Gus. The warmth of his gaze heating her skin made her want to get up and leave the room. If she didn't have Lucy in her arms, she might have done exactly that. Because Gus made her want things. Like a future she wasn't sure she was meant to have.

He'd endure another punctured lung if it meant an impromptu lunch date with Mia.

Sitting across from her at the Tide Pool, he pretended to read the laminated menu. Okay, perhaps that was a bit of a cavalier thought. Surviving the accident on the *Imogene* and being airlifted to the hospital wasn't an experience he'd care to repeat.

But this? A serendipitous morning spent almost entirely alone with Mia? Yeah, he'd vote for more of that. Dean had been right. Following her orders and avoiding air travel had granted them more time together. She'd driven him around town again this morning. First, they'd dropped off Poppy at a parents' morning-out program hosted by volunteers at a local church. Then she'd taken him by the clinic, where Dr. Baldwin had extracted the chest tube. Goodbye, annoying medical device.

Hello, beautiful.

She caught him staring. Her eyebrows lifted. "Have you decided what you're ordering?"

He set down the menu on the table. "Fish sandwich and fries. You? Wait." He held up one finger, then leaned forward to scan the menu again. "I predict you're a soup-and-salad-combo kind of girl, aren't you?"

Two appealing spots of pink shaded her cheeks.

After hanging out with her for a little over a week, he was getting good at predicting her behavior. Which made him only want to know more about her.

"Their chowder is incredible." Her eyelashes kissed her skin as she glanced down at the menu.

"That's what you order every time, isn't it?"

"Maybe."

Their server approached. He was a young guy in his midtwenties, with his sandy blond hair pulled back in a bun. He had on an orange T-shirt with the Tide Pool's logo on the front, jeans and a black half apron tied around his waist.

He turned to Mia with this pen poised over his notepad. "What can I get you today?"

Her mouth twitched like she was trying not to laugh. "May I please have a cup of clam chowder, house salad with honey mustard dressing on the side? Oh—" She gave Gus a pointed look. "I'd like to add an order of French fries, please."

"Excellent." The server turned to Gus. "And for you, sir?"

"Fish sandwich with fries, please."

"Perfect. I'll have that right out for you."

"Thanks." Gus handed him his menu. The server collected Mia's menu then moved on to the next table.

"How about that, you ordered a side of fries. Way to walk on the wild side."

Mia sat back in the booth. She slid the silver rings stacked on her right ring finger up and down. Up and down. "I like order. Structure. It's comforting to know what I'm getting into."

A long pause hung in the air. Around them, the subtle hum of conversation ebbed and flowed. The restaurant phone rang and a server passed by with a tray loaded full of food. He couldn't tear his gaze from Mia's. Something had shifted between them. Or had he imagined that? Either way, sharing a meal without Poppy or any of Mia's family around made him feel bold. What did he have to lose by asking everything he wanted to know?

"Am I correct in assuming you aren't dating anyone?"

"What?"

"Unless you're in a long-distance relationship or dating someone who doesn't care that you're spending all of your spare time with me, I—"

"I'm not spending all my spare time with you."

"You're spending at least half of your day off with me."

"True."

"I feel it's safe to assume you're single. Am I right?"

She unwrapped her silverware from the napkin and aligned it on the table. "You are correct. I'm not dating anyone."

"Have you dated anyone since Abner passed?"

"A couple of guys. Nothing serious." She collected her hair in her fist and pulled it over one shoulder. He tracked her movements. Even that one casual gesture made his fingers itch to run his hand through her hair.

"Why are you asking about my personal life?"

"Because I want to get to know you better."

Because I want to know if you'll ever get over him.

Yeah, that would cross an invisible line.

"I think it's only fair that I get to ask you the same question."

"All right." He tilted his head to one side. "Ask away."

"Are you single?"

"One hundred percent."

"Have you dated anyone since you got divorced?"

"I dated someone last summer." He hadn't thought of the woman since they'd parted ways last September. "She was only in Dillingham temporarily, which was for the best, because she had no interest in Poppy. I could never be with someone who didn't like my daughter."

Mia's face softened. "She's a sweet little girl, and so fun."

"I couldn't agree more."

"What's your favorite thing to do together?"

Gus settled back in the booth. "Oh, so many things. She loves animals. When the weather is decent, we get outside to play as much as possible. I try to tell her about everything we see, because I want her to be more verbal. Communication with a toddler can be frustrating sometimes. I'm dreading the day she can speak in sentences, though, because I think she'll ask a thousand questions."

Mia tipped back her head and laughed, allowing Gus an unrestricted view of her slender neck. The delicate silver earrings with a trio of glass beads dangled from her perfect earlobes. What would it be like to plant a kiss in the tender space under—

"Gus?"

Heat flared on his skin. "Sorry. I got distracted. What was the question?"

"Asher, my brother-in-law, is a wildlife biologist. If anyone knows about animals on the island, it's him. Want me to ask if he knows of anyplace that we could take Poppy this time of year?"

We. He liked the sound of that. "Poppy would love that. Thank you."

She reached for her phone. "Let me text him."

While she sent Asher a message, Gus glanced at a flyer tucked in a metal coil beside the condiments on their table. Local Little League baseball season started soon. The small piece of paper announced tryouts, which were being held at a field named after Abner. Gus frowned. The guy was like a chaperone at a party—hovering along the wall, but always quick to intervene when the fun ramped up.

Or Gus flirted with Mia.

He wasn't about to speak ill of his best friend, especially since he was no longer around. Abner had been passionate about so many things, including baseball. They'd named a field after the guy. Jealousy gutted him. How would he ever convince Mia to move on if Abner's memory always lingered?

She liked Gus way too much for her own good.

The bits and pieces of his questionable past faded from her memory as they sat in the middle of lunch rush at the Tide Pool. His face lit up when he talked about Poppy. She'd been able to resist handsome men who flirted, but the devoted-single-dad vibe was pushing her to the edge of her limits. The way his eyes held hers when he flirted made warmth blossom behind her sternum. And, boy, had he flirted.

Their server arrived with their lunch, saving her from thinking about the corded muscles rippling under his skin as he unbuckled his sling. A blessed distraction, her soup-and-salad combo.

"Here's ketchup for those fries." Their server set the bottle in the middle of the table. "Can I get you a refill on your drinks?"

"More iced tea for me, please." Mia took her napkin and spread it on her lap.

"I'm all set. Thanks." Gus offered a polite nod then draped his discarded sling over the back of the booth.

Mia squeezed ketchup onto her plate of fries then passed the container to Gus.

"What do you like to do in your free time?" He created a pool of ketchup on his plate, then dipped a fry and popped it in his mouth.

She hesitated.

He groaned playfully. "Mia, please tell me you have at least one hobby."

"I used to bake. I called it stress baking, and I'd give almost everything I baked to my sisters, or I'd leave it in the break room at work."

"Why did you stop?"

"My kitchen is still being repaired from the water damage."

He paused, his sandwich halfway to his mouth. "Your parents have a great kitchen. I'm surprised you're not baking up a storm."

She angled her head to one side. "Are you saying I'm stressed?"

He gave her an are-you-kidding-me look before he took another bite.

"Yeah, you're right. I'm stressed." She stabbed a slice of carrot with her fork.

Why did she struggle with work-life balance?

Chewing thoughtfully, she savored the crisp, sweet taste of her salad.

Gus dug in his pocket, then produced a small plastic bag containing pills. "Time for my midday medication."

She nodded her approval. "Between research to keep up with my mother's health issues, plus trying to keep an eye on the repairs at my house and working full-time, I haven't had the energy for much else."

"You forgot the time you're spending with your handsome new friend, Gus."

He flashed a smile over the rim of his water glass, which only added more fuel to her wanting-what-she-couldn't-have fire. Heat flared on her skin. Hadn't she just listed the reasons why she didn't have any spare time? So why bother daydreaming about the possibility of a relationship?

Because he's devoted and strong and an amazing father. Because you're so tired of being lonely.

She gave those unhelpful thoughts a mental shove.

"You can wipe that smug smile off your face anytime now."

"No, I don't think I will." His grin stretched wider, if that was possible, creasing the lines around his eyes. "You didn't argue with me when I identified as handsome, so I'm going to be a radiant beam of sunshine for the rest of the day."

"Good. Happy to hear I can help boost your self-confidence."

Averting her gaze, she crumbled crackers and dropped them into her chowder. They ate in comfortable silence. Her mind wouldn't stop spooling with thoughts of Gus. *People changed, right?* He seemed much different than the guy who'd staked his reputation on being the life of the party.

She hadn't corrected Gus when he'd mentioned his physical attractiveness. Women seated nearby had sent plenty of appreciative glances his way. She'd have to be dead not to notice. The chemistry between them was almost impossible to ignore.

Why not reconsider?

Because her whole life would be upended if she fell for him. Nothing about her career or his hometown or their commitments to their families had changed. Besides, he'd already told her he fully intended to get back on a fishing boat as soon as he could. His expression grew serious. "What kind of research are you doing to help your mom?"

"I keep up with clinical trials for new medications that might be coming on the market. If she needs radiation or chemotherapy, I've contacted some of my friends who work in oncology for recommendations on the best cancer-treatment centers."

His eyebrows knitted together. "Why would she need chemo or radiation?"

"Aplastic anemia can sometimes be treated like leukemia."

"Where would she have to go?"

"Seattle, or possibly Houston." Mia dipped her spoon in her chowder. "Obviously, we'd go with Seattle because it's the closest."

"Will your dad go with her?"

"No, I'd go with her. Dad builds houses so he doesn't usually like to leave the island for long, especially during spring and summer."

Gus stopped chewing.

"If I need to, I'll take a leave of absence from work, rent a studio apartment or a room in somebody's house while Mom gets treatment."

"That's quite a commitment."

"She's my mom. The one who raised me, anyway. Even if we're not genetically connected, I love her with my whole heart. I'll do anything to help her get well."

"Have you given any more thought to contacting your biological parents?"

She set her spoon back in her soup. "I'm not ready. I have wondered if they're curious about me, but Lexi hasn't shared hardly any details about them. What if they're angry that the mix-up has been discovered? What if they don't want to meet me?"

Gus reached across the table and blanketed her hand with his. "Then that's their loss. Your love for your family is remarkable, Mia."

His kind words paired with the rough callouses of his fingers against her knuckles sent her heart rocketing into orbit.

"Mia and Gus?"

Oh, no. Abner's parents stopped beside their table. Abner's mother, Tracy, stared in horror at their intertwined hands. Her husband, Colin, stood behind her, his hand on her shoulder. His face reflected barely concealed anger.

"It's not… We're not… It isn't what you think." Mia stumbled over her words. "We're not together."

"Colin. Tracy." Gus gave them a polite nod. He slowly caressed the back of her hand with his thumb. She resisted the urge to kick him. He was making this so much worse.

Mia pulled free and fisted her hands in her lap. "It's great to see you again."

Tracy's face pinched. "I wish we could say the same."

Anger zipped through her veins. Occasionally, she and Abner's parents crossed paths.

They'd meet in the aisle at the grocery store, or when they both had to mail a package at the post office. Their families didn't socialize together anymore. Tracy and Colin both saw Dr. Rasmussen for their health-care needs.

"Colin and I deserve a warning before you parade your romance all over town." Tracy's voice grew louder, drawing customers' attention from other tables. "At the very least, you could have called and told us you were dating."

"All right, honey. Let's go." Colin steered Tracy away from the table. Tears glistened in Tracy's eyes as she spoke to him, gesturing with both hands. Colin guided her out the door. Standing on the sidewalk, she fell into her husband's arms. He gently rubbed her back as her shoulders shook.

Mia pushed away her unfinished meal. She wasn't hungry anymore.

"Don't let her get to you." Gus kept his voice low. Those amazing blue eyes glittered with fierce determination. "It's been almost *four years*. You have every right to prioritize your happiness over Colin and Tracy's sorrow."

Did she, though? She hated that her actions had made Tracy upset. "We should go. You have to pick up Poppy soon. She needs an afternoon nap, right? After I drop you both off at the house, I'm going to go into work for a few hours. There are some charts I need to catch up on."

His jaw tensed. "If that's what you want."

"Yes, that's what I want." She reached inside her purse and pulled out her wallet then flagged down the server and requested the check.

While they waited, Mia scrolled through her phone until she found Tracy's number. She quickly typed out an apology then deleted it and started again. Colin and Tracy had been very special to her. She'd never in a million years intentionally hurt them. She had to make this right. Gus was not her boyfriend. Today's lunch wasn't even a date. Tracy and Colin had shown up at the worst possible time. They'd caught them in a tender moment. But that's all it was. Nothing more.

Chapter Eight

Being bored and alone was not good for him. The previous version of Gus Coleman would've used the scenario as an excuse to get into trouble.

But he wasn't that guy anymore.

Now he had a daughter to consider, which meant he had to figure out how to get another job. What if crabbing season ended before he fully recovered from his injuries? When Mia had first shared the news that he was a liability at sea, he'd scoffed at her prognosis. Since a week and a half had passed and he'd endured the pain of his recovery, he recognized the wisdom in her decision to keep him grounded.

He swiped at some errant crumbs on the kitchen countertop with a damp paper towel. If only he could swipe away his restless feelings so easily. After plucking a cookie from the package he'd left open in the pantry, he tucked the flap closed and moved it to a different shelf. The dishwasher hummed, and clothes tumbled in the dryer in the laundry closet down the hall. He'd attempted a few chores, but Dean had ended up taking over because there wasn't much Gus could do with his limited range of motion.

Yet another example of how his current circumstances would conspire against him if he wasn't vigilant.

He wanted to see Mia again. Alone. Lunch today had been nearly perfect, until Colin and Tracy had shown up and flipped out. Mia's guilty expression didn't sit well. He wanted another chance to caress the soft skin on the back of her hand. Remind her that Tracy didn't get to dictate Mia's future. He'd do just about anything to come up with an excuse to invite her over.

Since he couldn't be with Mia, he'd have to reroute his focus into his job search. He'd bought a new phone and Dean had helped him draft an email to a friend who ran a crabbing operation back in Dillingham. Through the grapevine, Gus had heard from a couple of his crewmates that this captain, a buddy from high school, was offering jobs through the end of the season. That was only four and a half weeks unless the season was extended because the crabbers didn't reach their quotas. An extension would add another two weeks to the season and maybe even allow him to get back on a boat.

His chest and shoulder throbbed, like tiny warning bells reminding him that he wasn't anywhere close to being ready. He had almost no ability to function on his own. But he knew this captain and his reputation for offering guys work when they needed it most. At the very least, maybe Gus could work in the warehouse, supervising the crew and prepping the lines and crab pots.

He checked his email for the fifth time. The guy hadn't responded. Gus scrolled back and reread the message, double-checking that he'd included his new phone number. Everything his friend needed to reach him was in the message.

Gus blew out a long breath. There had to be something he could do. Even after his body was completely healed, Mia probably wouldn't be thrilled about him getting another job as a crew-member. He wasn't ready to say goodbye to crab fishing though. He'd loved the work for so long. The thought of starting over with a new career planted an icy ball of fear in his gut. There was no way he'd let these injuries win. He'd get better. He had to get better. Because what choice did he have?

After setting his phone on the coffee table, he prowled around the guesthouse again. Poppy hadn't made a peep. She'd happily eaten her dinner. Dean had helped her with her pajamas, and Gus had read her two stories. Then she'd gone to bed without a fuss. Dean had reconnected with a high-school buddy who worked in Hearts Bay, and they'd decided to have dinner at Maverick's and watch a college-basketball game on TV. Now all Gus needed was a reason to reach out to Mia.

He turned and studied her parents' house. Darkness shrouded the property, except for a subtle glow from his porch light. The main house obstructed his view of the driveway, so he couldn't tell if Mia had returned for the evening. She'd mentioned working this afternoon to catch up on her charts. Had that been an excuse to leave the Tide Pool? Or did she genuinely have work to do? Ever since they'd hung out at the community-center playdate yesterday and shared lunch together today, he couldn't stop thinking about her.

Sometimes the chemistry between them felt almost palpable. The lingering glances. Subtle smiles. Not to mention he hadn't been able to look away when she'd held her niece in her arms. Her tender expression, followed by the wistful regret that flashed in her eyes when he'd asked if she wanted to be a mother, had wound its way into his heart. As always, thoughts about Mia and her future brought back reminders of Abner.

And that made Gus feel so very guilty.

Yes, he'd told her that Tracy and Colin didn't get to dictate her plans. But the hurt and disgust etched on their faces had made his heart pinch. Chemistry and lingering glances weren't a solid foundation for a meaningful relationship. Especially if her heart still belonged to Abner.

He pressed his fingers to the window's cool glass and stared out into the night. When would he be able to kick these feelings of inadequacy? There was nothing he could do to change the past. He knew this down deep in his core. So why couldn't he move on?

If a relationship with Mia was out of the question, he was going to have to find a way to deal with these relentless feelings of attraction. Because they were only growing stronger. Maybe he needed boundaries. Less time spent around her meant less opportunities to daydream about what could never be.

The muffled hum of a notification on his new phone pulled his attention from staring out the window. He crossed to the sofa, pushed aside a magazine and found his phone trapped between the cushions. A text message from Mia greeted him.

Can I stop by? I have extra food from friends at church and news about scheduling your lab work.

He didn't even hesitate. Texting with one hand was a challenge. Thankfully, the preset options made responding easy. Maybe too easy.

Sure, come on over.

He sighed, then tossed the phone back on the cushion. So much for boundaries.

What was she *doing*?

Mia stood shivering outside the front door of the guesthouse, her hand poised to knock.

She had a shopping bag full of disposable containers, filled with homemade cookies, a salad and a casserole from friends at church. Word had spread about her mom's deteriorating health and the water damage at her place. Folks in Hearts Bay were always so kind to step up and help whenever a crisis developed. She and her family were all very grateful for the meals that had arrived at their doorstep. They had more than they could possibly consume. Surely, Dean, Gus and Poppy wouldn't mind having a few meals. She needed to speak with Gus about scheduling his lab work, anyway.

Before her courage vanished, she knocked on the door.

The food and scheduling are excuses. You just want to be with him.

She acknowledged the thoughts as they spooled through her brain, then quickly dismissed them. Gus was the only person in her life that gave her his undivided attention. Her concerns about his past behavior, the countless ways he'd let people down and stories she'd heard about his wild nights partying in town, had all vanished. None of that mattered now. His insistence that Colin and Tracy's loss shouldn't influence her future had stayed with her all afternoon. She'd apologized to Tracy but hadn't received a response yet.

The dead bolt turned with a deliberate *thunk*.

Her heart kicked against her ribs.

She stared at the door, willing it to open.

Gus greeted her from the other side.

He smiled and her stomach plummeted faster than an anchor being dropped from the deck of a boat. How could he possibly look more handsome than he had this morning? Despite the frigid gusts swirling around their legs, he was barefoot, and wearing faded jeans and a well-loved T-shirt with the University of Alaska logo in the center. The forest-green cotton hugged his broad shoulders and emphasized his athletic torso. His short hair was damp and perfectly tousled. The ruddy glow on his cheeks looked especially appealing. Her gaze slid to his clean-shaven angular jaw. He had ditched the sling and for a second he looked almost healthy again.

She held up a shopping bag. "I brought over some food. Did you eat dinner already?"

Gus nodded. "Poppy's in bed and Dean's out with a friend at Maverick's. I'm not one to turn down food, though. Come on in."

"Thanks." She stepped inside and he closed the door.

After slipping off her boots, she padded into the kitchen and started unpacking the bags. "We received quite a few meals. More than any of us can eat. I thought you guys might like this chicken-and-rice casserole. There's also a salad and some chocolate-chip cookies."

"Sounds great. We'll eat that tomorrow. Thank you." Gus stood close enough that she could smell the appealing scent of his aftershave.

Stay focused, remember?

Standing here with his broad shoulder nearly brushing against her and that fragrance teasing her… Well, it was enough to make her forget why she'd stopped by. She went to the refrigerator and put the casserole and salad inside. "May I leave the container of cookies on the counter?"

"You may," Gus said. "Or we could eat them. Would you like something to drink? I have milk, tea or decaf coffee?"

"Decaf coffee sounds great. Thank you."

After they fixed their hot drinks, Gus led the way back into the cozy living room. He settled on the sofa. She sat down next to him, making sure there was plenty of space between them.

"Oops, I forgot to grab the cookies," Gus said. "Would you mind?"

"Of course not." She set her mug on a coaster on the coffee table then returned to the kitchen. A package of napkins sat beside the sink. She snipped open the plastic and pulled out a small stack. Adding the napkins to plastic container of cookies, she went back into the living room.

Her steps faltered.

In the short time she'd been in the kitchen, Gus had managed to light the trio of white pillar candles arranged on a square plate on the side table. The glow from the candles mingled with the flames crackling in the fireplace. A tendril of steam curled from her coffee.

Gus met her gaze, and his mouth tipped up in that half smile she was finding increasingly more difficult to resist.

"Perfect," he said, his eyes dipping to the cookies she clutched in her hands.

"Uh-huh." She barely breathed out the word as she skirted the end of the sofa and slowly sat down.

Wow, she was in trouble. If she hadn't been feeling so needy, she probably would've abandoned the cookies and coffee, shoved her feet back inside her boots and made a quick exit back to her parents' house.

But she didn't want to leave. She wanted to sit by the fire and talk to this strong, empathetic man who'd known more than his fair share of heartache. After lifting the lid off the container, she set the cookies between them on the table, then reached for her coffee again. They could do this. They could have an ordinary, uninterrupted adult conversation.

Right?

Gus's new phone hummed on the table. He eased forward and glanced at the screen. "Excuse me a second."

"No problem." Mia grabbed a cookie and took a bite. The sweet flavors of sugar and chocolate exploded in her mouth.

Gus jabbed at the screen, then frowned.

Mia polished off the cookie then took a sip of coffee. "Is everything okay?"

"Yeah, I need to answer Liesel's text and it's awkward with one hand."

"Anything I can do to help?"

"Want to text my ex-wife for me?"

Mia shrugged. "Sure. What do you want me to say?"

He passed her the phone. "Let her know that Poppy and Dean are here and Poppy's doing just fine. The less info we share, the better. Liesel likes to offer unsolicited advice and that's...not a great scene."

Mia dusted the crumbs from her fingers, set her mug on the table, then took the phone and quickly composed a text. "How's this?"

Gus leaned closer and glanced at the screen. "Perfect."

Mia hit Send. "Done."

His fingers brushed against hers as he took the phone. A pleasant warmth zinged up her arm.

"Thank you." He smiled. "Is there anything you don't do well?"

Mia picked up her coffee and settled back against the cushions. "You're very sweet. I'm terrible at lots of things."

"I don't believe that for a second," Gus said. His phone hummed again in his hand. He glanced at the screen then sighed.

"Need me to send another message?"

"Nope." Gus set the phone facedown on the table. "She'll try to keep the conversation going for the rest of the evening, asking questions, dropping passive-aggressive hints about things she's certain I'll forget to do for Poppy. It's maddening."

Mia studied him. Questions about Gus and his previous relationship drifted through her mind. "If you don't mind my asking, what happened? Why didn't your relationship work?"

"We had very different expectations about what healthy communication in a marriage looked like." Gus shifted, angling his body toward hers slightly. The flames in the fireplace spilled golden light into the room, painting the planes of his face. Mia tucked up her legs underneath her.

"Neither one of us grew up with parents who modeled loving, committed relationships. Liesel wants to control everything because that's how she learned to cope. I want to avoid conflict because that's how I survived childhood. My dad was dangerous and unpredictable. He—" Gus hesitated, staring down into his coffee.

Mia reached out and touched his arm. "You don't have to tell me anything you don't want to."

His eyes flitted toward her hand, still pressed against his forearm.

She pulled away, cradling her coffee with both hands.

"I want to tell you. It's part of who I am."

"All right."

"My dad abused my sister multiple times. I should have been there to protect her."

How awful. Her body flushed hot, then cold. "You were just a kid. How could you possibly have intervened?"

"I was physically strong enough that I could have done something about it. Dean… He didn't want me to get hurt." Gus paused. The muscles in his throat worked as he swallowed. "Dean and Carina bore the brunt of the abuse. I felt so guilty that I hadn't protected my sister, hadn't put a stop to what our father had done, that I was a mess emotionally. My dad's in prison for the rest of his life, and that's something I'm afraid I'll be dealing with for the rest of mine."

"Oh, Gus." Her heart ached for all that he'd endured. She'd been so insensitive. So ignorant. "I'm sorry."

He met her gaze. "You don't have anything to be sorry for."

"But I do. I've misjudged you and said things to you that I had no business saying."

"You were right about some of it. I was reckless. There's something about being irresponsible and playing with fire that intrigued me. A sick, twisted kind of survivor's guilt. But when Abner and Charlie passed away and I was supposed to be on the boat with them, that really nudged me into a dark place."

"I know. I remember."

"After their accident, I didn't feel like I deserved to live."

Mia winced. "That was a dark time for all of us."

"But my mom made sure we went to church and to youth group, and even though she was certain none of that stuck, somewhere deep inside I knew I had a purpose. Liesel came along at a time when I should've steered clear of a relationship. My wild behavior didn't change much, and she got tired of trying to fix me. Not that it was her responsibility to begin with, but in the beginning she secretly liked having someone who was more of a project than a partner. It wasn't until we had Poppy that I started taking my relationship with the Lord seriously. By then, Liesel didn't want to be married. I think she regretted becoming a mother, to be honest."

"Oh, that is so sad. Poppy is fortunate to have you."

"I'm doing the best I can. Figuring out as I go along, you know?" He leaned forward slowly and set his mug on the table.

"That's all most of us are doing." She took another sip of her coffee then set her mug beside his. Sitting here by the fire with Gus, the space between them crackling with attraction, she was too nervous to eat a second cookie.

"Can I ask you something?"

Her pulse thrummed. "I—I guess."

"Did you really come here to talk about lab work and to deliver a meal?"

She tucked a strand of hair behind her ear. "That's part of the reason. Why do you ask?"

His eyes darkened to a very appealing shade

of blue. Slowly, he raised his arm and cupped her cheek with his palm.

She sighed then leaned into his touch. Somewhere in the back of her mind, warning bells chimed. His gaze roamed her face. She couldn't look away.

"Because ever since you walked in here, I got the distinct impression you had something else on your mind."

"Such as?" The words left her lips as a breathy whisper. Her heart pounded so loud she was certain he could see it pulsing in her throat.

His gaze dipped to her lips. Every inch of her wanted to lean forward and claim his mouth with her own. But was that what he wanted?

"I really want to kiss you right now, Mia." The gruff texture in his voice made her insides dip and sway.

"Good, because I want you to."

He barely waited for her to finish speaking before he closed the distance between them. She shut her eyes and let her hands find their way gently along his forearms until she gripped his wrists. His mouth explored hers. Feather-soft at first. Then he deepened the kiss. Gus tasted of chocolate and coffee, and she couldn't get close enough.

He was kissing her. Finally. He'd envisioned this moment so many times and now that it was happening, he didn't want it to end. She smelled like flowers and citrus, and tasted like choco-late-chip cookies. Her skin was so soft beneath the pads of his thumbs. Her silky hair spilled forward and brushed against his arm. Slowly, her fingers released from his forearms and gently slid up to cup his biceps. He never wanted her to let go.

Everything good and perfect about the moment shattered when she suddenly pulled back. "We can't."

His heart pounded in his chest. "What's wrong?"

She scooted away from him. "This is so not a good idea."

Her words landed like a sharp left hook. "Why not?"

He'd been doubly sure to ask permission. Ever since she'd walked in tonight. Scratch that, ever since he'd landed in the ER when she was on shift, he'd been attracted to her. All of their interactions had led to this.

Why was she bailing now?

She stood and strode into the kitchen, coffee mug in hand.

"Mia, wait. Don't go. Not like this," he called after her, slowly pushing to his feet.

Water splashed in the sink as she rinsed her mug, then returned to the living room.

He scrubbed his hand over his face, desperate to come up with the right words to persuade her to stay.

She moved toward the door without looking at him. That kiss had been incredible. But just as he feared, it scared her. Scared him, too. Because he'd already gone and messed up a good thing. Why had he let this happen? He rubbed his palm against the tightness burning in his chest.

Mia shoved her feet into her boots. "I shouldn't have come here. This was a huge mistake."

Her words knifed at him. "No, please don't say that."

He couldn't move, could barely force out the words as she shrugged into her coat, then zipped up the front. Gathering her long hair in one hand, she quickly pulled it free from her collar. He tracked the path of her hair as it cascaded over her shoulder.

"I'm sorry, Gus. I really appreciate you being here for me when I needed someone to—" She stopped abruptly and shook her head, then pressed her palms to her cheeks. "What have I done?"

His disbelief morphed into anger. Was this about Colin and Tracy? "We didn't do anything wrong, Mia."

Her face fell. "Don't you understand? You have a daughter and a life on the other side of the state. I have family drama and a job and people depending on me. You work in one of the most dangerous professions in the world. We're all wrong for each other. I'm sorry. I didn't want to hurt you."

Yeah, too late.

He bit back the words and braced his aching arm against his chest. He'd learned from dealing with Liesel not to say anything else to set a woman off. She'd clearly made up her mind. So what could he possibly come up with to persuade her to stay?

It was time to retreat. To pull up stakes and move on. That's what he'd always done and what he'd do again so he didn't get hurt. Because he was so tired of hurting.

"Good night, Gus." Moisture shimmered in her beautiful eyes, then she turned to leave.

"See ya."

Okay, maybe a little rude and dismissive for someone he'd just kissed. But it was all he could muster before she slipped out and closed the door quietly behind her. He hesitated, then shame and regret washed in.

Coleman, you're an idiot. Don't let her walk away.

Panic propelled him across the room. He grabbed the doorknob, but his steps faltered. Wait. He'd already promised himself he wouldn't beg. What was he going to do? Run out into the night and ask her to come back?

How pathetic.

He let go of the knob and pressed his forehead against the door. The cool metal soothed his hot skin. *Lord, how did I botch this? Please show me how to fix another broken relationship.*

The muffled sound of Poppy crying out in her sleep turned him down the hallway to the room where she was sleeping.

"It's okay, sweetheart." He smoothed damp wisps of hair from her forehead. "Daddy's here and you're okay. Go back to sleep."

She wedged her thumb in her mouth. He nestled her stuffed animal under her arm, covered her back up and left the room.

Dean came through the front door, a proud smile on his face. "I just passed Mia getting into her car. Right on, dude."

"Ha. Not even close, pal." Gus sank down on the sofa cushions and reached for his sling. His shoulder was on fire.

"What happened?"

"Nothing. Everything. I don't know, man." Gus scrubbed his hand over his face. "I thought she wanted me to kiss her. So I did, and she jumped up and ran out of here like her socks were on fire. I've messed everything up. Again."

Chapter Nine

Maybe a wedding reception wasn't the best way to reconnect with her friends.

Mia stood in front of Hearts Bay's new waterfront hotel. The one that had replaced the restaurant her sister Eliana had managed for years. Nostalgia curled around her, warm and comforting, like one of Grandmother's crocheted blankets. She'd spent hours with her sisters in the café's corner booth, enjoying long talks and extra servings of dessert. They'd mourned the loss of Harbor Lights Café due to an unfortunate fallen-tree incident, and a challenging dispute over zoning regulations.

But now she had to admit the new hotel and adjoining convention center were beautiful. Many happy couples had married and hosted receptions in the venue. Tonight, second thoughts kept her outside, stalling. The new

Mr. and Mrs. Sebastian Wilcox happened to be two of her closest friends. Sebastian and Abner had grown up together. When he'd met Brooke and they'd started dating, Mia had tried so hard to be happy for her friends. The families on the island who fished for a living were a tight-knit group. A community that she'd once been a part of. For some people, including Sebastian and Brooke, the people they fished with became their families.

Mia already struggled with a sense of belonging, even before Lexi had discovered the Maddens. Abner had been her person. The one she'd planned to spend her life with. He was a successful businessman, a loyal friend, a solid Christian and had a passion for Little League baseball. She had never imagined that they wouldn't build a future together.

Dipping her toe back into the proverbial pool filled with people who'd known them as a couple felt daunting. But if she was honest, she'd kept to herself for long enough. Staying home from this reception was selfish.

And she'd made far too many selfish choices lately.

Brooke and Sebastian had recently eloped to Mexico. Instead of a wedding, they'd planned a big party for their friends in Hearts Bay. Mia had been scheduled to work a seven-to-seven shift in the ER today. Dr. Calvert had covered an extra hour for her so she could leave early to change and get to the reception on time.

She stared at the building's entrance. Her hands tightened around her car keys tucked inside her coat pocket. It would be so easy to turn around and leave.

Overhead, stars filled the inky night sky. The wind blew in off the water, teasing a tendril of her hair that had slipped from her updo. She tugged it free then tucked it behind her ear.

"Come on, you can do this," she whispered.

Brooke and Sebastian made a lovely couple. In the past few years, most of her friends had gotten married. Started families. Some had even added a second child. She still saw them around town, waved from an opposite pew at church on Sunday and occasionally treated their illnesses or injuries at work. Being the only single one in a group of couples and families with young children had gotten painfully awkward. Maybe that would never get easier?

A car door slammed then a taxi eased away from the curb. Footsteps approached from behind. She turned around. Gus.

He stopped a few feet away. His piercing gaze made her breath catch.

They hadn't seen one another since they'd kissed, and she'd fled. A solid twenty-four hours had done nothing to tamp down her frazzled emotions.

"Hi."

"Hi," he said. The streetlamps bathed them in a silvery blue light. His appreciative gaze swept over her. "You look stunning."

"Thank you. Y-you clean up nice, too."

Ugh. Why did she have to make this so awkward? She never stumbled over words like this. Only when she was with him. She tried not to let her eyes wander, but he did look handsome in his pressed black trousers and silky blue button-down. How had he managed to find clothes that fit him so well?

"Sebastian's brother brought extra clothes. He hooked me up." Gus angled his head toward the entrance. "Need a plus-one?"

She released a nervous laugh. "I'm surprised you're still speaking to me after last night."

A muscle in his jaw twitched. "You're the one who regretted the kiss, Mia. I, on the other hand, would kiss you again in a second."

Oh. Heat flared on her cheeks. She couldn't look away. "I appreciate your honesty. I'm truly sorry for hurting you."

"Apology accepted. Sebastian and I played basketball together growing up. He and Brooke mean a lot to both of us." He extended his elbow.

"What do you say? Friends don't let friends go to wedding receptions alone."

She tucked her hand in the crook of his elbow and they walked through the automatic doors of the hotel together.

A trio of artificial trees decked out in clear lights stood off to one side. A tiled entrance led to plush carpeting and modern furniture in the lobby. An attendant stationed at the front desk offered a polite smile.

A hand-lettered chalkboard sign in the lobby directed them toward the ballroom to the right. They followed the muffled sound of bass pumping through speakers. Through the propped open double doors, Mia caught a glimpse of Brooke and Sebastian in the middle of the dance floor.

The popular song had an appealing beat, and plenty of other couples had joined the newlyweds. Sebastian grabbed Brooke's hand, pulled it to his lips, then brushed a tender kiss across her knuckles. Brooke rewarded him with a radiant smile.

Mia's heart pinched.

Gus paused at the entrance. Concern filled his eyes. "Are you good?"

Had she gasped or said something out loud? "I'm fine."

"Are you sure?"

"Yeah, I just…" She trailed off, then forced a smile. "There are a lot of people here that I haven't seen in a while. I'm a little out of practice when it comes to wedding receptions."

His mouth tipped up in a gentle smile. "Same."

His kindness warmed her all the way to her toes. "I thought maybe you could relate."

"We need a secret password."

"Like a code?"

He nodded. "A word we can say to each other when we need to get out of a tough conversation."

"Oh, that's clever."

He lifted one shoulder. "I try."

She chuckled. "How about we use *Poppy*?"

"Works for me." He winked. "Let's do this."

Buoyed by Gus's concern, or maybe just the fact that he was beside her, offering his arm, she stepped confidently into the reception. They weren't five paces inside the ballroom before one of Hearts Bay's most gregarious women accosted them.

"Oh, my word, Mia Madden. Is that you?" Lindy, the wife of one of Mia's high-school classmates and Brooke's best friend, greeted her. Lindy was wearing a tiny red sequined dress, cherry-red lipstick and mile-high stilettos. She had to raise her voice to be heard over the music, drawing more than a few curious glances.

So much for confidence. "Hey, Lindy." Mia froze as Lindy squeezed her in a tight hug.

When she pulled away, Gus leaned down and spoke close to her ear. "I'm going to get you something to drink. Be right back."

His breath warmed her skin, sending goose bumps swirling around her neck.

Lindy clutched at the sleeve of Mia's jacket with her manicured nails. "Is that Gus Coleman? Good for you, girl. He is so-o-o-o good-looking!"

Wow, okay. Mia shrugged out of her coat and draped it over her arm. "Gus was one of the guys who survived when the *Imogene* sank. He's staying in Hearts Bay until he recovers."

"Mia, I didn't expect to see you tonight." Stephanie, the wife of another crab fisherman and Lindy's cousin, joined them. "How are you? It's been ages since we've talked."

"She's here with Gus Coleman." Lindy shot Stephanie a knowing look.

Stephanie's eyes grew wide. "I didn't realize you guys were together. How long has that been going on?"

"Oh, no. No, no, no." Mia waggled her hand at them like she was intervening between two middle-schoolers about to pull off a prank. "We're not...together."

"Really." Lindy smirked. "You walked in here very much looking like a couple."

"We're just friends."

"I thought he was married." Stephanie frowned. "Don't they have a child?"

Mia's spine straightened. She never should have come here. If she'd stayed home, she could be in her pajamas and devouring a pint of ice cream. It would've been so much easier to send Sebastian and Brooke a generous gift.

"He's not married." She forced out the words but refused to share any additional details about Gus's personal life. Now would be a good time to implement his exit strategy.

Stephanie shrugged. "My mistake. You know, I've got to say, Mia, I never thought I'd see you date another fisherman."

A sour taste coated the back of her throat. Could this conversation get any worse? Before she could mumble a reply, Gus was at her side, gently extracting her coat from her hands.

She stared at him. Without a word, he draped her coat over a nearby chair, then deftly placed a plastic cup of lemonade in her hand. "Sorry, no chai latte served tonight. This will have to do."

"Thank you." Her hand trembled as she took a long sip.

Gus rested his palm on the small of her back then faced Stephanie and Lindy. "Ladies, it's been a minute. Hope you're having a good time."

"Oh, my night just keeps getting better."

Stephanie grinned, her gaze sweeping from Gus's head to his toes and back again.

Gross. Mia drained the last of her lemonade. Gus was so close to her the hair on her arm stood on end.

"Are your husbands here?" Gus surveyed the room. "I'd like to say hello."

Mia resisted the urge to loop her arm around his waist. *Please, no*, she silently pleaded. *Don't leave me with these piranhas.*

The song ended and the DJ transitioned to a slow ballad.

Gus's brilliant blue eyes dipped to hers. His thumb caressed the fabric of her dress. "Dance with me?"

"Aww, that is so sweet." Lindy splayed her palm across her chest. "You two are adorable."

She didn't give Lindy or Stephanie the satisfaction of a response. She turned away and tossed her cup in the trash can behind her, then accepted Gus's outstretched hand. It was only one song. Besides, she had to get away from those two before they started talking about Abner and the dozens of shared experiences that had once composed their lives together.

Gus threaded his fingers through Mia's and led her onto the crowded dance floor. When she'd turned away, he expected her to toss her empty cup then keep walking right out the door. Now that they were free of Stephanie and Lindy's nosy questions and juvenile comments, he braced for her to pull her hand away and make an excuse to avoid dancing.

But she didn't. He forced his expression to remain neutral, but as she faced him, a flicker of hope reignited. He placed his hands on her waist. She reciprocated by resting her palms on his shoulders.

"Is this okay?" Her eyes roamed his face.

"More than okay." His voice sounded gruffer than he'd intended. She clearly had no idea how her proximity affected him. Dancing with a beautiful woman was something he hadn't done in a long time. Holding on to Mia like this made him feel invincible. All his pain and uncertainty faded into the background as they swayed together. The mirror ball overhead spilled pastel-colored lights like confetti across the ballroom.

Man, she was gorgeous. He couldn't stop staring. She'd styled her hair in a fancy twist, and her skin looked even more appealing than usual, offset by the emerald-green shade of her dress. Her palms warmed his skin through the thin fabric of his borrowed shirt.

He forced himself to look around the room. At least for a few seconds. Since he'd stepped out of the taxi and spotted her outside, he'd been silently praying he didn't say or do anything to mess this up.

A guy he used to fish with a few years back caught his eye and waved. Gus acknowledged him with a polite nod. There had to be close to two hundred people here. Add that to his list of reasons why he was shocked Mia hadn't left yet.

"Thank you for rescuing me." Mia stared at a spot somewhere over his shoulder. "I'd forgotten how intense those two are when they're together."

"You're welcome." They turned in a slow circle. He counted at least six people blatantly staring. He refused to pay them any attention. Given how quickly she had flipped from amorous to panicked the night before, he wasn't going to waste a single beat of the slow song getting distracted. He'd allowed other people's opinions to hold too much power over him for far too long. Many of the people attending the reception had probably seen him at his worst. He'd fished with these guys for years. Stayed out far too late on countless occasions and strived to be the most obnoxious dude in packed bars night after night.

But tonight, he reveled in their curious stares. Let Lindy and Stephanie blab to every guest that he and Mia had arrived together. Tonight he was dancing with the most beautiful, intelligent, kind-hearted human he'd ever known.

Even if the song only lasted for three minutes, it would be three minutes of bliss.

Mia tightened her grasp on his shoulders. The warmth of her body swaying near him, the sensation of her palms pressed against the sleeves of his shirt and the intoxicating fragrance that teased his senses all threatened to demolish his self-control.

His arms ached to draw her closer. He wanted to rest his cheek on her silky smooth hair and confess that he couldn't believe this had all worked out so well.

Sebastian had bumped into Dean at Maverick's. They'd struck up a conversation, then Sebastian had invited them to come to the reception. Dean had respectfully declined. Instead, he'd offered to stay with Poppy so Gus didn't have to scramble to find a babysitter. He made a mental note to thank Sebastian. Without his invitation, there's no way Gus would be holding Mia in his arms right now.

She tipped up her chin. Those gorgeous green eyes found his again. How could one simple look make him want to kiss her so badly? "You're a good dancer."

"We're barely moving."

"It doesn't matter." Her eyes dipped to his mouth. "You're confident. Attentive."

Oh, boy. He was in trouble. His eyes slid to

her delicate collarbone, exposed by the square neckline of her green velvet dress. Tiny cap sleeves and the rest of the formfitting dress emphasized her toned figure. One slow song was all he was going to be able to handle.

Dancing with Mia made his anxious thoughts about showing up here alone melt like a pile of snow in the warm spring sunshine.

"I was on the verge of saying something I'd regret to Stephanie and Lindy," she said.

"They're kind of like hungry wolves circling their prey."

Mia's mouth twitched as she tried not to laugh.

"I thought for sure you were going to bust out our code word," he said.

"It was touch and go there for a minute."

"Crisis averted." He took one of her hands and tucked it against his chest. "You're safe with me. I would never let anything happen to you."

Her expression sobered. He cocooned his hand over hers. Could she feel his heart thrumming in his chest?

"Mia? You know that, right?"

She bit her lip and looked away. "I—I know."

His scalp prickled. He tilted his head, urging her to look at him. "That wrinkle in your brow and the doubt in your eyes tells me maybe your heart doesn't agree."

"Gus, I—"

"Hey, you two." Sebastian and Brooke danced beside them. "We're glad you're here."

Mia's expression brightened. "Thank you for the invitation. Congratulations to you both."

"Congrats to the new Mr. and Mrs.," Gus added. He'd known Sebastian a long time and had never seen his friend look so happy. "Mrs. Wilcox, you're looking lovely this evening."

Brooke grinned. "Thank you, Gus. How are you feeling? So sorry to hear about the accident."

"I'm feeling much better thanks to Mia. She patched me up."

Mia shot him a playful look. "You're doing the hard work to get well. It has hardly anything to do with me."

Sebastian glanced from Mia to Gus. "I heard you're looking for work. Did you apply for a job on the *Zafiro*?"

Surprise flashed in Mia's eyes and her steps faltered.

Gus caressed the back of her hand with his thumb, but it did little to ease the tension that seemed to be coiled like tight knots in her muscles.

Don't. Please. Gus narrowed his gaze, silently pleading with Sebastian to stop talking.

"If the captain needs a reference, have him

call me." Sebastian grinned. "I'll tell him you're the best around. Maybe you'll get—"

"Come on, man," Gus interrupted him. "Nobody wants to hear us talk shop tonight."

"I'll make it quick." Sebastian twirled Brooke around again so he could speak to Mia. "Gus will be a huge asset to that crew. The captain of the *Zafiro* is a legend. He likes to take risks, but they'll hit their quota and be back in port before you know it."

Gus stifled a groan.

Mia stopped dancing. "What did you say?"

All the color had drained from her face.

"Uh-oh." Brooke's worried gaze flitted between Mia and Sebastian. "Baby, I don't think you should've told her that."

They stood in the center of the dance floor. The music played on.

Sebastian's smile faded. "Didn't Gus tell you he'd applied?"

Gus fought to keep his anger contained. "Sebastian, stop talking. Please."

Mia stared up at him. Accusation flared in her eyes. "You want to crew on the *Zafiro*?"

He offered a pathetic nod.

Sebastian glanced from Mia to Gus and back to Mia. "I'm so sorry, Mia. I thought you'd be happy for Gus. Crab fishing is his life."

"I know. That's the problem." Her chin wobbled. She slipped from Gus's arms. "Thank you for inviting me tonight. Congratulations. I've got to go."

She weaved between the couples on the dance floor, plucked her jacket from the chair, then ran from the ballroom.

No. For the second time in two days, he watched her walk away. This time he wasn't going to let her go without pursuing her.

He hurried outside. "Mia, wait."

She ignored him. Her high heels clicked across the asphalt outside the hotel as she stormed toward the parking lot. The tails of her long coat flapped against her bare legs.

"Mia, we have to talk about this." Gus picked up the pace, cutting long strides down the sidewalk. He still wasn't in any shape to run, but he was determined to catch up with her before she got in her car.

At the corner of the building, she whirled and faced him.

Her breath came in short gasps. Moisture clung to her eyelashes. "The *Zafiro*, Gus? Really? Everyone knows that captain runs a dangerous operation."

"Give me a minute, okay? I can explain."

"Please do. I'd love to hear how you're going to spin this."

"You're right. In the past, that boat had a

sketchy reputation. But the captain's made some changes recently, and I'm trusting that he'll follow safety protocols and hire a reliable crew."

Mia jammed her hands on her hips. "Sebastian just said he's a risk taker."

"Sebastian's a good guy. I'd trust him with my life. But he doesn't always think before he speaks."

Her mouth opened and closed, then opened again. "Were you ever going to tell me?"

Anger surged through his veins, fierce and hot. "Does it matter?"

"Yes."

"No one's offered me the job yet. I'm hoping to hear something soon. Getting back on a boat before crab season ends has been the goal all along. So help me understand why you're upset."

Her eyes turned flinty. Her beautiful features morphed into a protective shield. "Because I've already lost my brother and a fiancé to the sea. I'm not interested in losing anyone else."

She turned and walked away.

He leaned against the building, staring out across the harbor. Security lights mounted on posts illuminated the boats docked in their slips. The familiar silhouette of commercial fishing boats with their nets neatly spooled, awaiting their next run, usually filled him with a sense of anticipation. He belonged out on the water.

Pursuing the next catch. Battling the elements. Pushing his body to the edge of its physical limits.

Somewhere, metal clanged against metal, in a sad, lonely rhythm. A hollow ache settled in his core. Did his work really mean anything at all if he didn't have a woman he loved in his life? He'd wanted desperately for that woman to be Mia. But was it fair to ask her to love someone who fished for a living when she'd already endured two catastrophic losses?

Chapter Ten

"Mia? Have you ordered Mr. Allen's CT scan yet?" Taylor, Mia's medical assistant, hovered in the hallway outside Mia's cubicle. She held up a sticky note. "I know we've been swamped, but this is the second message he's left."

"I'm so sorry." Mia rifled through the stack of papers on the counter until she found her notepad with her list of things she had to do. How had she forgotten? "I'll order it now."

Taylor hesitated, her brow furrowed. "If you don't mind my asking, is everything okay?"

"Of course." Mia forced a smile. "Why do you ask?"

"You seem...really distracted, that's all."

"Thanks for asking, but I'm fine. Great, actually."

"Right." Taylor smoothed her hand over the ends of her long platinum-blond ponytail. "I'll bring our next patient back."

"Perfect." Mia gestured toward her electronic tablet. "I'll order Mr. Allen's CT scan."

Poor Mr. Allen. Such a sweet man. Mia hated that her oversight had impacted him. She had no one to blame but herself.

And Gus.

Admittedly, she wasn't an expert on first kisses. Since Abner passed away, she hadn't dated anyone she'd liked enough to go on more than two dates. Hence, the lack of kissing. Even from her out-of-practice viewpoint, an incredibly romantic encounter like the one she'd shared with Gus in the guesthouse two nights ago was supposed to make her feel lighter than air. Or spring backflips down the hallway. Instead, after Sebastian and Brooke's reception she'd tossed and turned from midnight until 2:00 a.m., alternating between crying and praying for wisdom. Why had he not told her about applying for a job on one of the most notorious crab-fishing boats?

And why was she so angry with him for doing what he loved to do? She'd gone to church yesterday then watched one of her favorite movies with Rylee at her place. They'd shared a pizza for dinner. She'd managed to avoid Gus. Nothing about her thoughts or emotions regarding a relationship with him seemed any clearer this morning. What was she supposed to do now?

But the hurt in his eyes, his words and his rigid posture—those details were almost as difficult to ignore as the way she'd felt when he'd kissed her.

Oh, brother. So ridiculous. One kiss and a sweet slow dance were not supposed to tilt her whole world into chaos.

After placing the order for her patient's diagnostic test, Mia abandoned her post and strode down the hall to the medical clinic's front desk. She discreetly peeked into the waiting room.

A chorus of sniffles, coughs and a fussy baby greeted her. Every seat was full.

"Wow, we're slammed again today." She'd already treated two ear infections and a case of bronchitis. It wasn't even ten in the morning yet.

Joan, their receptionist, reached for the ringing phone. "I need to work in another patient on your schedule before lunch."

Mia hesitated. "I'm already seeing ten people."

"Sorry, Mia." She scrunched her nose. "Every provider is overbooked by at least two patients."

"All right. Add them in."

The woman nodded then picked up the phone. "Hearts Bay Medical Clinic. This is Joan, how may I help you?"

Since that nasty stomach virus had ravaged the island, a bit of a reprieve would be a blessing. Mia sighed then returned to the tiny alcove she used as a makeshift office. She'd stay late today to finish her charts and tackle that to-do list. Usually she looked forward to covering a rotation in the clinic. She approached an overbooked schedule as an obstacle to conquer. But today was not that day. Her eyes were scratchy from lack of sleep. Stress from the past few weeks had turned her back and neck into a mass of tight muscles. Kissing Gus had made everything about her life more complicated. Not to mention dancing together at Sebastian and Brooke's reception had reminded her of how good it felt to be part of a couple.

Except finding out he was returning to work scared her. Yes, Gus was right. Helping him get well so he could work again had always been the goal.

But she still wasn't ready to see him go.

She didn't want to love someone who had almost drowned but was more than willing to get right back on another fishing boat.

She checked the time on her watch then crossed the hallway to the break room. Taylor needed a few minutes to screen the next patient. Plenty of time to fix a cup of coffee.

"There you are." Dr. Baldwin strode into the room, opened the fridge and retrieved a bottle of sparkling water. "I just had a second appointment with a patient that you originally treated in the emergency room. Gus Coleman."

The small packet of creamer Mia had opened slipped from her hand and spilled on the counter.

"Oops. Sorry. I didn't mean to startle you." Dr. Baldwin opened the water bottle. "I wanted to give you an update, since Mr. Coleman appears more than ready to leave the island."

Blood roared behind her ears. Almost two weeks had passed since the accident. More than likely he'd recovered enough to travel. She avoided her coworker's gaze and fumbled for a napkin to wipe up the spill. "H-how is he?"

"Looks good, all things considered. I pulled the chest tube last time I saw him. The extraction site is healing nicely, and his heart and lungs sound great."

"Excellent."

"I've ordered follow-up X-rays." Dr. Baldwin took a sip of his drink. "His progress note from the physical therapist is encouraging as well."

"That's wonderful." She infused her voice with optimism and dumped another package of creamer into her coffee. "Glad to hear he's feeling better."

"Like I said, he wants to leave the island. I recommended the ferry, but he says he's traveling with a young child and prefers to fly. He'd benefit from additional visits with a physical therapist in Dillingham, but I'm having trouble convincing him of that."

"So you've cleared him to fly?"

He swallowed a sip of his water. "If his chest X-ray is normal and he can tolerate the discomfort."

"Right." Mia stirred her coffee, determined to keep her expression neutral.

"Do you disagree?"

Thoughts of Gus's hands cupping her face and his lips on hers spooled through her mind. Heat rushed to her face. "No, I—I trust your judgment. Thanks for the update, Dr. Baldwin."

"No problem. Have a great day." He left the room, whistling an upbeat tune.

How embarrassing. He'd kindly shared an update and asked for her opinion, and she couldn't stop blushing because she'd kissed the patient and danced with him one time.

Mia blew out a long breath then topped her coffee with a plastic lid. Gus wanted to leave the island. Dr. Baldwin had cleared him to fly. That kind of news was worth celebrating.

But that kiss had muddled her thoughts, because now the idea of saying goodbye made her sad. She'd gone and done the very thing she'd said she'd never do again. She'd fallen in love with another fisherman.

* * *

Gus stood in the exam room at the medical clinic, impatiently waiting for the assistant to return with his discharge paperwork. Mia's muffled voice filtered through the closed door. She was here. Out in the hallway. His pulse sped. He stared at the door, willing her to knock and then step inside.

She'd offer him his paperwork and pretend that was the reason she'd popped in. Then those beautiful green eyes would lock on his and she'd bite her lip before confessing her feelings. She'd admit that their epic kiss had scared her. Prompted her to run off. But now she realized that her anger about Sebastian's comments had been misplaced.

Her voice grew louder as she moved closer.

Gus stood still. The familiar sound of her laughter wound around his heart. He kept his eyes trained on the door. Sure, she probably had a hectic schedule. But he wanted to believe that she'd still make time for him. That she cared enough to want to clarify her behavior with a deeper explanation. Fabric rustled, footsteps slowed, then someone knocked on the door.

"Come in." He barely choked out the words.

The door opened and the medical assistant who'd helped him stuck her head inside. "Here's your discharge paperwork and more information about stem-cell donation, Mr. Coleman."

She smiled then slid some papers onto the counter beside the sink. "Someone will contact you about your lab work. You're all set. Safe travels."

"Thanks." He offered a curt nod then turned away, his hopes deflated. So much for anticipating an apology. Mia couldn't even be bothered with saying hello. Maybe her decision to let Dr. Baldwin handle his care was all the confirmation he needed. As much as it hurt, maybe he needed to call the moment.

Mia was still angry, and she wasn't interested in a serious relationship.

He'd done his part. Followed up like she'd told him to. Paid attention to Dr. Baldwin's advice. Agreed to repeat X-rays. He'd even moved forward with the stem-cell-donation lab work. The assistant had said she'd make sure the sample made it to the lab in Anchorage.

Gus reached for his jacket and gingerly put it on. His shoulder and collarbone still throbbed if he moved the wrong way. If he identified as a potential match, then he'd help Mrs. Madden. He'd keep his word.

But that didn't mean he had to stay on the island and wait for the results.

Dean had already offered to fly with him and Poppy back to Dillingham. Their mother had called early this morning from New Mexico and shared that Grandpa was doing well. Since she had hired a caregiver for him, she planned to return to Alaska in the next few days. Gus sensed that Dean's visit to Alaska and the news that Carina's pregnancy had become high-risk had motivated Mom to come home sooner.

Gus grabbed the sling he no longer needed, along with the paperwork, and stepped out into the hallway. There wasn't much he could do to help his sister, but he'd feel better knowing that their mother and Dean were both back in Dillingham. He didn't want to be the reason Carina and Jeb lacked reliable help. They could all work together to care for one another. Because that's what healthy families did. His time here in Hearts Bay had reminded him what it meant to be a part of a family. How important it was to look out for loved ones.

Pausing, Gus glanced back down the hallway. A woman in blue scrubs and a white jacket with a sleek auburn ponytail stepped into a room and closed the door.

"Checkout is this way, sir." A young blond woman with a nametag labeled Taylor pointed in the opposite direction. "Someone at the front desk can help you."

"Thank you." He turned and slowly walked toward the exit sign. His visit had been a success. He got what he wanted—medical clearance to fly. That stupid tube and sling were gone. Even though the doctor who'd helped him had forecast a long road to a full recovery, Gus had his freedom back.

He couldn't shake the nagging sense of disappointment, though. When he'd rolled into the ER on a gurney, writhing in agony, he'd never imagined he'd be walking out of the clinic two weeks later with Dr. Baldwin's blessing. His recovery never would've happened without Mia and her family caring for him. He longed to share the good news with her.

But she'd known he was here. Right? And she didn't behave as though she cared. His phone buzzed with an incoming text. While he waited his turn in line, he read the message. Dean wanted him to know he and Poppy were in the parking lot.

Gus checked out, then left the clinic. Outside, a cold rain fell, stinging his cheeks. Hunching his shoulders, he hurried across the wet parking lot toward the truck Dean had borrowed from Asher. Yeah, it was time to go. The captain of the *Zafiro* had offered him a job this morning, and he'd accepted the position. If there were seats on tomorrow's flights, he'd get Dean to book them. Because he had no reason to stay.

Wow. Okay, this was really happening. Mia paced her living room. She'd finally nailed down a time to connect with Lexi. This call was long overdue. Lexi had been extremely patient. Still, the fact that they were even talking because they'd been switched at birth made Mia's stomach churn.

She didn't want to do this. Everything about this situation made her sad and angry. If her family wasn't really her biological family, what anchored her here? Yes, as a Christian, she'd always been taught that her identity in the family of God gave her a solid foundation. But she was only human, and Lexi's arrival in her life had shaken her to the core.

Sidestepping an industrial fan and a neat stack of boxes filled with supplies for the contractor, Mia glanced at her phone again. Two minutes until their scheduled call. She'd decided to chat with Lexi from her own house, even though it was in disarray from the water damage and ongoing repairs. Thankfully, the crew had taken the day off and the house was empty and silent. Exactly what she needed right now.

Her heart kicked against her ribs and she took a quick sip of water. Then her phone played the familiar chime of an incoming video call. Mia answered. A beautiful young woman's image filled the screen.

Mia's breath caught. Lexi's features resembled Tess's and Rylee's. "H-hello."

"Hey." Lexi's smile wobbled. "Are you Mia?"

Mia formed her mouth into a smile. "Yes. You must be Lexi."

"It's so nice to finally meet you. Thank you for taking the time to speak with me." Lexi dabbed at the corner of her wide-set dark brown eyes with a tissue.

Mia's throat tightened. This had to be an emotional moment for Lexi, too.

"How are you?" Lexi's Southern accent was charming. She'd clearly put some effort into applying her makeup. Her dark hair spilled across her shoulders in a waterfall of bouncy curls.

"I'm okay. A little nervous, to be honest." Mia tucked a loose strand of hair behind her ear. She'd had a hectic day at the clinic and hadn't bothered to check her appearance in her car's visor mirror before she raced over here to take the call.

"Me, too." Lexi wrinkled her adorable button nose in a gesture so like Rylee that Mia couldn't help but do a double take.

"Oh, my. That expression. You are most definitely a Madden." The words slipped out of her mouth, and she quickly pressed her fingertips to her lips. "You have my—your—sister's ability to scrunch up your nose."

"Thank you." Lexi sniffed and dabbed at her eyes again. She splayed her hand against her pink sweater. "You have no idea what it means to hear someone say that. I—I hope I'm a Madden. Based on the information I've gathered, I believe that I am. But there's a possibility that we've got this all wrong and—"

"No." Mia shook her head. "I don't think you need to worry about that."

Lexi's eyes filled with empathy. "This can't be easy for you."

"Thank you for acknowledging that." Mia propped her phone against a stack of books on her shelf and burrowed her hands in her jacket pockets. "I never imagined I'd be having a conversation like this."

"This is very kind of you to invite me into your life. Especially since it seems you had no idea I existed," Lexi said.

"None."

"Believe me, I thought long and hard before I reached out." Lexi angled her head and the pink-and-cream beads on her dangling earrings shimmered. "This is the kind of news that can rock somebody's world."

"How does your family feel about this?"

Lexi hesitated. "Not great. They're in denial, I believe. My father also suspects that the online DNA analysis I used is inaccurate."

"It's challenging information to absorb," Mia said. "Aunt Sheila, Dad's sister, submitted her

DNA sample because she got the kit as a Christmas gift. She's since confessed she was afraid to share the results with us."

Lexi's eyes widened. "That's how the database linked me to y'all."

Mia shivered. Aunt Sheila's confession had upset her parents. This was hard. On everyone involved. She regretted taking this call alone. "Is there anything I can help you with? Any questions I can answer?"

"Well, I've finalized my plans to visit. My husband won't be able to come. He's in the military and can't take leave right now. But I bought my ticket last night." Lexi grinned and clapped her hands. "I'll be there on April twenty-first."

Oh. Mia tried to keep her disbelief from creeping into her voice. "You've already bought a plane ticket?"

"I found a deal that was too good to pass up. Besides, I want to get there a little early so I'll have plenty of time to see the island and meet everyone before the commemoration."

Ten days early? She didn't know what to say.

"Oh dear. Did I say something wrong?" Lexi frowned. "Y'all will tell me if I'm overstaying my welcome, right?"

"You're traveling a long way. It makes sense that you'd come early and get used to the time change." Mia willed her facial expression not to betray her raw, honest feelings. She wasn't ready to meet Lexi. Or for Lexi to meet the whole family. The fact Mia had several weeks to get used to the idea didn't lessen her anxiety at all. Everyone would happily welcome Lexi into their lives, even if her mother had to tow an IV pole and an oxygen tank.

But nothing could emotionally prepare Mia for Lexi's arrival in Hearts Bay.

"Do you have any recommendations for a place to stay?" Lexi glanced down, then flashed a notepad with a neat list toward the camera. "I found a bed-and-breakfast, a hotel and a lovely resort online. Is there a specific place that you'd recommend?"

Mia hesitated. Their parents would say Lexi had to stay with them. Rylee and Tess would probably insist on it, too. Gus wouldn't be around in April, which meant the guesthouse would be vacant. "My family, I mean your parents…" Mia trailed off, pressing a palm to her forehead. "This is so awkward. What I'm trying to say is, you're more than welcome to stay with us."

"Are you sure? Is that something everyone will feel comfortable with?"

"If you need your space, I can give you some recommendations."

"No, I'd be thrilled to stay with family if you're confident that works well for everyone."

"I'll double-check. If for some reason it's not going to work out, I'll let you know."

"Thank you for your generous offer. I would love to stay close by, if it's not too much trouble."

"You're welcome. Can you text me your flight info and we'll plan to meet you at the airport?"

More words she wanted to take back as soon as they left her mouth. She had no business offering to play hostess when she knew full well that Lexi's arrival was going to be incredibly difficult to handle. Guilt slithered in, making her feel like a hypocrite. They exchanged more awkward small talk, then ended the call.

Mia heaved a sigh then slumped onto her sofa. What a surreal conversation. Her phone buzzed with an incoming text message. Expecting it to be a follow-up from Lexi, she went back to the bookshelf and grabbed her phone. A message from Rylee filled the screen.

We're having dinner with Gus in an hour. He says he's leaving the island. Dean and Poppy are flying out with him tomorrow. Are you coming over to say goodbye?

Mia reread the message. Tomorrow? She'd suspected Gus would leave, but part of her had hoped it wouldn't be so soon. Selfishly, she'd longed for more time to sort out her complicated feelings.

No thanks. I'm at my house. Think I'll stay here and get a few things done.

Her phone made that not-so-satisfying whoosh as she sent her reply to Rylee. Wasn't she supposed to feel good about herself for staying strong? Sharing a meal with Gus around her family's table would only fill her with more regret. More reminders of what could never be. He had to provide for his daughter and needed a job. She wouldn't ask him to change careers, but she couldn't afford to trust him with her heart.

Chapter Eleven

"More?" Poppy sat on the floor at Gus's feet, playing with a mixing bowl, a wooden spoon and a set of measuring cups. She held up her empty sippy cup.

"You may have some water." He pointed toward the implements in her hands. "Why don't you make more soup?"

He took the cup from her. She studied him, then went back to stirring her imaginary soup. Gus blew out a breath, grateful that he had another excuse to look out the kitchen window.

"Are you sure you packed all of Poppy's things?" Mrs. Madden was sitting at her kitchen table, holding a mug of hot tea. Purple circles darkened the skin under her eyes. She looked more fatigued than when he'd sat beside her at dinner last night.

"Dean's making one last pass through the

guesthouse to make sure we packed all our stuff." Gus smiled at Mrs. Madden. "Thank you again for everything. I don't know what I would have done without you and your family."

And without Mia. He filled Poppy's cup with water and looked out the window above the sink. Still no sign of Mia's car pulling in the driveway. He'd been so disappointed when she didn't come over last night. Now he feared she wouldn't bother to say goodbye.

"We're more than happy to help." Mrs. Madden used the side of her hand to smooth some overlooked crumbs on the table into a neat pile. "People have helped us through hard times over the years. We're only paying it forward."

Gus leaned against the counter beside the refrigerator. "I'll be waiting to hear if I can be of any help to you."

"Oh, really? In what way?"

"I started the process to see if I'm a donor match."

Her eyes welled with tears. "Gus, that is so thoughtful. I don't know what to say."

He winced. "I didn't mean to upset you."

"No, these are happy tears." She produced a tissue from the pocket of her cardigan sweater, then dabbed at her eyes. "We're praying that something changes soon, especially now that we've found out about Lexi. I really want to get well so I can be a part of her life."

"Makes sense." He didn't know what else to say. Regardless of Mia's unwillingness to speak to him now, he wasn't about to betray her confidence. It wasn't his place to tell Mrs. Madden that Mia was wrestling with complicated feelings about Lexi and her plans to visit Hearts Bay. Gus checked the time on the microwave's digital clock. Asher would be here in a few minutes to drive them to the airport. His stomach tightened. He couldn't wait around for Mia much longer.

The front door opened then closed. Gus's breath hitched and he straightened. Maybe that was her.

"Hello?" Asher called out.

Gus sagged back against the counter. Definitely not Mia.

"Good morning, Asher." Mrs. Madden pushed to a stand. "Want some coffee or tea?"

"Good morning. Please don't get up." Asher held out both palms, his brow creased with worry. "I have coffee in the car."

"Oh, okay." Mrs. Madden slowly sat back down. She grimaced then pulled her sweater tighter.

Gus tracked her movement. "Do you need a blanket or anything?"

"No, no. I'll be fine." She waved him off. "You get packed up."

"We can start loading bags if you're ready." Asher's gaze flitted toward Poppy. "Want a hand with her car seat? Those things can be a beast to wrangle."

"Please." Gus glanced down at the items scattered around Poppy. "Dean should be here shortly with his bag. I'll get Poppy ready to go."

The front door opened again. Asher glanced behind him. "Hey, Mia. What's up?"

Gus's mouth went dry. She was here. Mrs. Madden winked at him over the rim of her mug before she took a sip. Warmth climbed his neck. He really didn't want to say goodbye to Mia in front of an audience.

"I'll get the car seat installed." Asher gently patted Mia's shoulder as she stopped beside him in the kitchen doorway.

"Right. Thanks," Gus said, his eyes already locked on Mia's. Asher could've suggested he was on his way to fill the car with angry weasels and Gus would've agreed. Mia's arrival had robbed him of all logical thought.

"Good morning." Her tight smile and the pain that flickered across her face made his scalp prickle.

"Hey," he said. "Thanks for stopping by."

She shifted her attention to Poppy.

"Zoop!" Poppy spotted Mia and held up an empty measuring cup.

Mia glanced at Gus, her brow furrowed.

"She's making soup," he explained.

"Ah, I see."

Poppy stood and toddled toward Mia.

Mia sank to her knees on the kitchen floor and greeted her with a wide smile. "Good morning, Poppy."

"Try?" Poppy thrust the measuring cup into Mia's hands.

Mia took the cup and tipped it to her lips, then made an exaggerated slurping noise.

Poppy giggled.

"Wow, that's the best chicken-noodle soup I've ever tasted." Mia patted her stomach then handed the cup back. "May I please have more?"

Poppy released a stream of gibberish, then reached for the cup and returned to her mess of implements scattered across the floor. She dropped everything into the large stainless-steel mixing bowl, then carried it back to Mia. Her laughter mingled with Poppy's. Watching the two of them play make-believe, Gus just about melted into the floor. He'd be nothing but a puddle if this kept up for much longer.

After he'd been admitted at the hospital, he was so angry when Mia had insisted he couldn't leave. Staying on the island was the last thing he wanted to do, but then he'd spent two weeks with Mia and her family… Well, mostly Mia. Especially Mia. Now he hated that he had to go. When he watched Mia and Poppy together, he felt like the biggest fool in the world for wanting to go back to Dillingham.

Poppy reached up and set a plastic lid on top of Mia's head.

Gus waited, expecting Mia to put a stop to Poppy's antics. Instead, she pulled a silly face and sat still, careful not to let the lid slip. Poppy squealed and tried to add the measuring cup on top of the lid. Both slid from Mia's silky hair and fell on the floor.

Mia picked them up and tried to balance the lid on Poppy's head. Poppy screeched and plucked it off. Gus and Mrs. Madden exchanged glances. He pretended not to notice the concern in her eyes, but he knew what she was thinking because he was thinking it, too. His feelings for his late best friend's fiancée had blown right past the physician-assistant-and-patient boundary.

The way Mia had cared for his life-threatening injuries, invited him into her family's home against her better judgment and patiently played with his daughter had all reminded him that she was an incredibly special woman. He wasn't an idiot. He knew he didn't deserve her. Even though they'd shared a moment and a kiss he'd never forget, it was probably for the best that their relationship hadn't progressed to something more substantial.

Because people he loved often got hurt. Even though he had no intention of hurting Mia, it seemed like it was inevitable with him and his relationships. But that still didn't stop him from wanting her. Because despite all his missteps and heartache, he wanted desperately to be loved.

"Good morning!" Rylee strode into the room. She quickly surveyed the scene. "Dean's outside with Asher. The bags are loaded, and Asher said you all need to get going."

Gus gently took the kitchen tools from Poppy and set them on the counter. "We're coming."

"I'm going to make my way outside, too." Mrs. Madden stood. "I want to say goodbye to Dean."

"Do you need help?" Mia offered, pushing to her feet.

"No, I can make it." Mrs. Madden moved slowly, her hands trailing across the backs of chairs. "Don't you worry, I'll put on my coat, too."

"Good." Mia retrieved a wooden spoon from the floor. "I was about to remind you."

When Mrs. Madden had left the room, Rylee

flashed Gus a knowing smile. "Want me to help Poppy get in the car?"

Her subtext wasn't hard to miss. *So you two can say goodbye.*

"Please." He handed Poppy's backpack to Rylee. "Thank you."

Mia glanced up at him. That familiar tightness lingered around her eyes. Maybe this goodbye wasn't going to be easy for her, either.

"Come on, Poppy." He held out his hand. "It's time to go."

The little girl's eyebrows scrunched together. "Go?"

"Yep. We're going to get on a plane, then fly back home."

"Me back home? See Mommy. See Mommy!" Poppy hopped up and down.

Gus rubbed his fingertips across his forehead. He didn't want to talk about Liesel. Or even think about her, to be honest. Thankfully, Rylee intervened.

"That's a cute snowman you have on your shirt, Poppy. Let's get in your car seat." Rylee leaned down and lifted Poppy into her arms. Poppy kicked and squealed, then reached for Mia.

"I'll see you later, sweet girl." Mia gave Poppy's leg a gentle pat. "Thank you for playing with me."

Rylee shifted Poppy higher on her hip and turned to leave. "I'll give you two a minute."

She left the house and closed the door behind her. Gus's heart hammered. He wiped his sweaty palms on his jeans. There was so much he needed to say.

"I'm sorry I didn't tell you about applying for the job on the *Zafiro*."

Mia faced him, her arms linked across her chest. "When do you start?"

He palmed the back of his neck. Was she even going to acknowledge his apology? "I'm starting out on land working in the warehouse. As long as my shoulder's feeling good, I'll hopefully be fishing by the end of next week or the week after that."

She tucked her hands inside the pockets of her green jacket. "Great."

A heavy silence blanketed the space between them. "Mia, I—"

"Gus, you don't owe me an apology or an explanation. I would never ask you to give up crab fishing or uproot your life in Dillingham for me."

She wouldn't? He swallowed hard. "But what if I wanted to uproot my life for you?"

Pain flashed across her features. "Please don't say that. You'd never be happy doing anything besides fishing."

"Isn't that a choice I should get to make?"

"I'm not asking you to choose." Her chin wobbled. "This is what you wanted—to finish out the crab season and provide for Poppy."

Was she blinking back tears? He forced himself to step away. Ouch. Her words gutted him. He left the kitchen and walked outside. Did she think not asking him to choose between her and his job somehow made this easier? Why hadn't their time together meant anything to her?

Asher had the engine running and he was drumming his fingers on the steering wheel. Dean sat beside him. Gus opened the back passenger door. Poppy's wails filtered toward him.

He turned around. Mia stood behind him. Moisture clung to her eyelashes. He pressed a kiss to his fingertips then touched his fingers to her lips. "I'm not giving up on us. I'll be back. I promise."

She clasped his hand in hers and squeezed. The longing mixed with sadness in her eyes tempted him to pull her into his arms. They held on for the last second until he let go then climbed in the car.

She closed his door for him.

"Wow," Dean said. "That was quite the goodbye."

Gus held Mia's gaze through the window.

"Are you ready?" Asher asked.

"Just go."

Before I change my mind. Gus didn't look away until Asher had pulled out of the driveway. Mia clearly had her doubts, but he wasn't giving up. He'd meant what he'd said. He'd find a way to come back to her and keep his promise.

That was the most romantic nonkiss of all time.

Mia stood in the driveway, her fingertips on her lips, staring after Asher's taillights. Her skin still tingled from Gus's touch.

Oh, brother. She had it bad. Why had she pretended that his leaving didn't bother her? He'd offered another glimpse of his tender, vulnerable side, and she'd panicked, then pushed him away. Even though she hadn't dated anyone in eons, the longing in his eyes when they'd stood in the kitchen had been unmistakable.

And like a fool, she'd let him leave. Trampled all over the possibility of a future together.

They'd come a long way since that horrific night in the ER when she'd worried she might not be able to stabilize him. Her concerns had been valid, yet Gus had recovered in record time. Now he was leaving the island and it nearly broke her heart. Stupid Dillingham. Why did it have to be so far away?

Sure, she could visit. But he hadn't invited

her. Why would he, now that she'd basically told him to leave? Her attraction toward Gus battled the logical parts of this messy puzzle. He'd said all along that he needed to get back to work, and his ex-wife wasn't making life easy in terms of caring for Poppy. Yes, he'd said he'd be back. When though? Between his plans to return to work and her demanding job, she couldn't fathom how they'd make plans to reconnect.

But she'd be lying if she said a piece of her heart hadn't just driven away in that vehicle. She'd always taken pride in being fiercely independent. Now she hated the notion of facing whatever was in front of her without Gus's strength to lean on.

The wind kicked up, swirling around her legs. She shivered, then gasped as a cold rain pelted her. Yanking her hood over her head, she held it in place and darted across the yard. She pushed open the front door and hurried inside.

Mom had fallen asleep on the sofa. Rylee was in the recliner, scrolling through her phone. She glanced at Mia. Her expression grew serious. She rose and crossed the room.

"Oh, no. That was a tough goodbye, wasn't it?" Rylee whispered.

Mia nodded, tamping down the emotion rising in her throat. She slipped out of her jacket and hung it on a hook nearby.

"Come here." Rylee draped her arm across Mia's shoulders. "It's going to be okay. This will all work out. You'll see."

"He said he'd be back and he wasn't giving up on us, but I was an idiot and pretended like I didn't care if he chose his job over a relationship with me."

Rylee pulled back. Disbelief etched her features. "I'm so confused. What's going on? I thought you cared about each other."

"I thought so, too." More hot tears pressed against the backs of her eyes. "We kissed, and danced at Sebastian and Brooke's reception, but then Sebastian let it slip that Gus wanted to work on the *Zafiro* and I flipped out."

Rylee frowned. "Why?"

"Because Gus just recovered from life-threatening injuries. Now he's pursuing another terrifying job and he's going back out on a boat. What if something terrible…?" She trailed off. She couldn't bring herself to even say the words out loud.

Rylee patted Mia's back gently. "Ah, I get it. You're not worried that he isn't coming back for you, you're worried that his life will be in danger and you'll lose him."

Mia winced. Rylee's words provoked more

pain. Like someone had pressed on a fresh bruise. Mia tugged off her shoes, left them by the door then pushed past Rylee. How had her sister diagnosed the problem so easily? Was she that transparent?

Mia retreated to the kitchen, immediately regretting her decision. Evidence of Gus and Poppy still lingered. The items she and Poppy had played with together sat inside the mixing bowl on the counter. Mia picked up the bowl, set it gently in the sink, then added dish soap.

Rylee leaned against the counter beside the sink. "Am I right?"

Mia refused to make eye contact. She turned on the water. If only she could scrub away the memories of Gus and his daughter.

"I told myself I wouldn't fall for him." Mia turned off the water and started washing the measuring cup. "He was Abner's closest friend, not to mention a crab fisherman, and I've already lost two people I love to that stinking ocean."

"You have every right to be concerned about his profession."

"But?"

Rylee pulled a dish towel from the drawer and held out her hand. Mia passed her the clean measuring cup. "Gus seems like a great guy. He loves to fish and wants to be a good provider. He appears to be a devoted father, too. I know this is less than ideal timing for you to start a new relationship, but why not give the guy a shot?"

"Because I'm afraid."

There. She'd said it. Put the truth out there for Rylee to overanalyze.

"We've covered that already." Rylee returned the measuring cup to the drawer. "Your fears are valid."

"Thank you."

"Hold on, I'm not finished."

Great. Mia washed the remaining items Gus had left on the counter then dried her hands on a towel. She wasn't in the mood for relationship advice from her youngest sister. Rylee hadn't dated anyone for a significant length of time recently. She'd had her own issues with commitment. Mia pinched her lips together, refusing to lash out.

"I watched you play with Poppy, and the chemistry between you and Gus is unmistakable."

"Tell me about it." Mia squeezed her eyes shut and pressed her palms to her flushed cheeks, desperate to avoid rehashing any more details of their goodbye.

"I want you to be happy, Mia. You and Gus would be good together. Good for each other."

Mia opened her eyes. "No. We wouldn't. Besides, it doesn't matter now. He lives on the other side of the state, which might as well be Iceland at this point. Poppy needs to be close to her mother and her father, and I'm not leaving this island until I know Mom is going to be okay."

Rylee stood at the counter, her mouth agape. "All right then. You've made your point. Sorry I interfered."

"Thanks for listening. I'm going to go." She strode out of the room, grabbed her jacket and put her shoes on. Mom was still sleeping on the sofa. Rylee stayed in the kitchen. Her sisters meant well, but none of them knew how it felt to be in her position. Lexi's revelation had upended her whole world. They could all pretend that nothing had changed, but Mia couldn't ignore the truth. She wasn't a Madden. Piling more doubt and uncertainty into her life by starting a relationship with Gus wasn't fair. Not now. Maybe not ever.

Being back in his own space wasn't all that satisfying.

Gus transferred the wet clothes from the washer to the dryer, then quietly closed the door and pressed the button to start the cycle.

Their brother-in-law, Jeb, had picked them up at the airport. Then they'd stopped for groceries. Poppy had melted down in the produce section, so they'd paid quickly and hurried home, where she'd fallen asleep at the dinner table. Gus had carried her back to her bedroom about an hour ago. Since he'd tucked her in, she hadn't made a peep. What a trouper. Their trip had been uneventful, but including their layover in Anchorage, it had taken all day to get back to Dillingham.

Dean had gone over to Jeb and Carina's place for the evening. Their mother was scheduled to fly in tomorrow. With Poppy hopefully asleep for the night, Gus had at least a dozen things to do. Being able to use both arms again was a bonus. He'd promised himself he'd stay on task. No wallowing. Except he couldn't stop replaying his encounter with Mia in the driveway this morning.

After ten hours and almost a thousand miles between them, he regretted not kissing her goodbye. If she doubted that he cared enough to come back to her, would a more romantic gesture have swayed her at all? Maybe he'd let his emotions cloud his judgment. She needed somebody in her corner. A stable, loving man with a boring job who came home for dinner every night.

She'd been honest from the minute they crossed paths. A relationship with a crab fisherman who craved adventure was not an option. Her personal preferences and conservative treatment plan for his injuries had aggravated him at first. But during his time in Hearts Bay, he'd sensed her opinion of him had shifted into something more favorable. He'd tried to show her that he wasn't the same guy she'd known when Abner was still alive. Tried to show her that he could be what she needed. Tried to show her that she was who he wanted.

For a few minutes after he'd kissed her in the guesthouse, he'd almost believed that his efforts had worked. When she'd kissed him back, he was almost certain she'd fallen in love with him.

Almost.

Clearly, he'd called that one wrong.

Gus padded into the living room and sat down on the gray microfiber sofa. A basket of clean laundry awaited him. Before he folded another thing, he had to check his email. The captain of the *Zafiro* was supposed to let him know about his first day of work and send him a link to on-line forms he had to fill out. After pushing his stack of unopened mail to one end of the coffee table, Gus slid his laptop closer and tapped the power button.

Once he opened his email, the captain's message was the first that popped up. Uncertainty rippled through him. An image of Mia with tears brimming in her eyes resurfaced in his head.

What if accepting this job was the wrong decision?

Brushing aside the doubt, Gus opened the message and quickly scanned it.

Finally. He was going back to work. The thing he'd wanted most these past several weeks was finally his.

Well, the thing he wanted second after a relationship with Mia.

Somehow, he was going to have to find a way to move past their painful goodbye. There was nothing else he could do to change her mind, except be patient. He'd learned to trust the Lord to work out so many impossible circumstances, including sparing his life in that horrible storm. He didn't want to wait for Mia to choose him because what if she never did?

He rubbed his palm against the hollow ache in his chest. The old Gus would've reached for an unhealthy coping strategy right about now. Instead, he closed his eyes and prayed.

Lord, I hate not knowing what's going to happen next. Please help me to keep trusting in You. I believe You know what's best for me, and for Mia, too. If we're meant to be, please show us the way forward. Thank You for sparing my life, helping me recover and for this job opportunity.

He opened his eyes and shifted his attention back to the email from his soon-to-be boss. His concerns hadn't vanished after silently offering his honest prayer. He felt less worried, though. A sense of peace blanketed him, instead of the shame and regret he'd often carried after he panicked and tried to handle things on his own.

The details were all there. He'd work in the warehouse for a week, then get back on board a vessel. Rumors were still circulating that the snow-crab season might be extended into April, since the regulators reported the population was plentiful. That species wasn't quite as lucrative as the red-king crab, but he wasn't about to turn down a job. Two or three solid weeks of work would be a huge blessing and ease his financial concerns for the rest of the year. Dean and their mother had already agreed to team up and help care for Poppy and Carina's children. Another huge blessing. If not for their generosity, he couldn't swing three weeks of work, especially since Liesel was still out of town.

Gus carefully rotated his shoulders, assessing his pain. Not a hundred percent, but much better than a few weeks ago, when he could barely move without wincing. Hopefully he could count on his body to step up to the challenge. He responded to the email then completed the online forms.

He needed this job. Not because he had to prove that he could get back on a crab boat, although that was important. He had vowed he'd provide for Poppy, and failing his daughter wasn't an option.

If only Mia could be a part of this equation.

Despite his prayerful attempt to surrender control only a few minutes ago, part of him already wanted to snatch it back. He blew out an exasperated breath. Couldn't he be a devoted father and love Mia, too?

He hadn't admitted to anyone that he loved her. The long trip today had given him plenty of time to clarify his feelings. She'd lost a fiancé and a brother in a tragic accident. Her whole world had been turned upside down with the switched-at-birth discovery. He didn't blame her for being afraid, but selfishly, her rejection still hurt. No matter what he did he couldn't shake his lousy reputation. What if she was right? What if they weren't right for each other?

No.

He mentally chased away the doubts and fears that crept in. *You're better than this.* He reached for the remote control, turned on the TV and scrolled until he found a college-basketball game. He pulled a clean shirt off the top of the laundry pile then folded it.

Coming back to Dillingham and taking this job had been the right decisions. He'd thought about staying in Hearts Bay and finding something temporary, but he couldn't keep asking the Maddens to accommodate him. He felt less guilty relying on Mom and Dean for childcare, and it was better for Poppy to be in her own familiar space, anyway. Being far from Mia was the worst, but he was determined to wrestle his doubts into submission. Because he wasn't going to get over her.

Chapter Twelve

Two months had passed since Gus had left the island. Mia had never been more miserable. Sure, she'd filled her days with work, picking up extra shifts whenever possible. After the repairs on her house had been finished, she'd convinced Rylee to help her re-paint most of the interior.

But the stress of her job and the physical demands of a DIY home improvement project hadn't been enough to completely distract her. She missed Gus and Poppy so much.

Returning to the guesthouse was the last thing she'd wanted to do, so she'd procrastinated about getting the place ready for Lexi's visit until the last minute. Now Mia worked quickly to scrub all evidence of Gus, Poppy and Dean from the guesthouse. Dusting the living room was her final task. She ran a soft cloth over the flat-screen television. Rylee had dropped by earlier to put fresh sheets on the bed and clean towels in the bathroom. Tess had sent a few groceries over to stock the place with basic staples.

Lexi was scheduled to arrive in less than two hours on the evening flight. Mom had insisted that Lexi was going to stay in the house, ironically in the room that Mia had vacated when she'd moved back to her own place last month. Thankfully, no one had asked her to host their long-lost family member at her house. But Rylee and Tess must've convinced Mom to let the woman have a place to retreat, because here they were, prepping the guesthouse.

Satisfied that the cozy space was dust-free, Mia turned to leave. The abandoned yellow rubber ducky lying on the carpet beside the sofa made her breath hitch.

She'd tried so hard to sidestep all thoughts of the handsome crab fisherman, but reminders of Gus and his adorable little girl were all around her. The Trading Post, where they'd been together, the physical therapy clinic she drove by often and this sofa where they'd kissed. She trailed her fingers across the back of the cushions. That memory was still too delectable to ignore completely.

She picked up the rubber ducky then dropped it in the box of toys to return to Asher and Tess. Oh, how she wished Gus hadn't left. He'd been a fantastic listener through this whole complicated situation. If only he hadn't gone back to Dillingham already. She respected him for doing what was best for himself and his daughter. To be honest, she really had no reason to feel sorry for herself. She'd encouraged his departure.

Shame heated her skin. She scooped up the toys and strode to the door. What if she'd been wrong? What if she was what was best for Gus and Poppy?

Don't be so selfish. Besides, it's a bit late for that. You've already ruined any possibility of a relationship.

The scathing voice in her head left zero room for grace these days. Her fear about risking her heart hadn't softened, but her regret about her choices grew each day that she and Gus were apart. In her work, she could be confident. Bold. In emergency situations, there wasn't time to doubt her instincts. When it came to loving this particular man, she'd been a coward.

She glanced at the time on her phone then left the guesthouse. It would have been easy to bail on meeting Lexi at the airport. After all, they weren't genetically linked. This wasn't her sister coming to meet her biological family. Instead, she silently prayed for strength and courage. She was the one who had connected with Lexi and helped arrange this visit. Skipping the trip to the airport seemed thoughtless.

With the toys wedged on her hip, she picked her way across the yard. Darkness had crept in, shrouding the island in shadows. She circled the house and hurried toward the front porch.

The door swung open and her father stepped out on the porch, backlit by the lights from the living room.

"I'm here. The guesthouse is all clean. I know we need to leave soon." She formed her mouth into a smile. "Are you excited to meet Lexi?"

He didn't answer.

Oh, no. Fear cinched her insides and squeezed tight. "Wh-what's going on?"

"Nothing's wrong. I wanted to speak with you for a minute." Dad tucked his hands in the pockets of his gray slacks, the ones he only trotted out for church. He'd put on a sweater she'd never seen before and shaved, and his dark hair was still damp. Wow, he'd gone all out to meet Lexi.

Shivering, she tried her best to ignore the jealousy oozing in. "Can we talk inside? I'm freezing."

Dad stepped back. She climbed up the steps and went into the house. Asher, Tess, Cameron, Rylee and Mom were all standing in a circle. Tess held Lucy in her arms.

"Sorry to keep you waiting." Mia set down

the toys inside the door. When she straightened, Dad pulled her in for one of his trademark bear hugs.

"This is a nice surprise," she murmured into the soft fabric of his sweater. He smelled faintly of cedar and spice, a fragrance she'd always associated with her dad.

He pulled back then kissed her temple. "We love you always and forever. I can only imagine how difficult this must be for you."

His tender words were all the permission she needed. The barrier she'd carefully constructed to corral her big emotions broke. Conversation in the room stopped. Even Cameron paused his chattering.

"I—I'm sorry." Mia rummaged in her pocket for a tissue. "I don't know what's wrong with me."

"But you're a doctor. Why can't you know?" Cameron asked, eyes wide as he stared up at her.

"Cam, take it easy." Asher ruffled his hair then whispered in Cameron's ear. He nodded his head and swallowed hard, then glanced up at Mia again. She offered him a wobbly smile. What a sweet kid. If anyone in the family could relate to her situation, it was Cameron. He'd had an interesting childhood, having found out in second grade that Tess, his reading teacher, was his mother. But she didn't want to commiserate with a preteen. The only person she really wanted right now was Gus. Sadly, crying on his shoulder was no longer possible.

"Come on, we should go." Mia lifted her chin and drew a deep breath. "Lexi's flight is going to land soon."

Dad's eyes shimmered with unshed tears. He cleared his throat. "I'm so sorry that this has happened, Mia. If I could, I would take all the hurt away."

"That's not your responsibility. You didn't cause this to happen."

"But your feelings matter, too," he said, his voice gruff. "My sister's the one who did the online DNA analysis and didn't share her results with us."

Their family filed out the door. Rylee walked beside Mom, supporting her elbow.

When they were alone, Mia reached out and squeezed her father's arm. "Aunt Sheila should've told us when she realized she had a relative in Georgia. But we can't change what's happened. Like I've said before, this could be the thing Mom needs." There was that stupid lump in her throat again. *Good grief, pull yourself together.* She had to be strong. Peaceful. Anchored. The wise older sister who didn't get her feathers ruffled.

"I'm worried about your mother's condition, but I'm also concerned that this has been hard on you."

Before she could find more words to reassure him, her phone chimed inside her purse. She pulled it out and glanced at the screen. The knot in her chest loosened as she read the message from Gus.

Thinking about you and your family. Hope meeting Lexi goes well.

She sighed. Why was he being so kind to her?

"Good news?" Dad asked.

She pocketed her phone. "A nice message from a concerned friend."

"Interesting." He winked. "I'm glad somebody special is thinking about you."

A few minutes later, they were all on their way to the airport. Mia drove and Rylee, Mom and Dad rode with her. They kept up a steady conversation and she tried to listen to one of her most inspirational playlists streaming through the sound system to keep herself distracted. Not because she was about to meet Lexi, but because Gus's words brought her comfort. Despite her best efforts to keep him at a safe distance, he'd found his way into her heart. She gripped the steering wheel tighter and fought to wrestle her feelings about him into submission. Even after she'd gotten angry with him at Sebastian and Brooke's reception, after she'd told him their relationship wasn't a possibility, he'd taken the time to send her message. She'd been selfish and afraid, and still he wasn't giving up.

What was she supposed to do now?

His kindness and concern didn't make her any less afraid. Only more regretful that she might've cast aside a good man who cared deeply for her.

His whole body hurt.

Gus unlocked his front door then stepped inside. This time, he was grateful for the silence that greeted him. Nudging the door shut with his foot, he tossed his wallet and keys on the side table then kicked off his boots. Yesterday marked eight weeks since he'd left Hearts Bay. It felt like eighty. Yes, he was grateful for his job. But it had been a rough transition. Engine trouble had kept the *Zafiro* in dry dock for longer than expected. He and the rest of the crew had stayed busy in the warehouse, attaching buoys to over one hundred crab pots. They'd reviewed their emergency plans multiple times. Finally, they'd tied knots in ropes and hauled groceries from the store to the warehouse. Trying their best to stay optimistic that they'd be able to leave port soon.

Gus had prayed hard for circumstances to change. With each passing day they'd been stuck in Dillingham, waiting for parts that kept getting backordered, he'd started to lose hope.

Then the new parts from Seattle arrived, the boat was repaired and finally they were underway. Less days to fish for crab meant less revenue. Their time-sensitive snow crab permit and the fact that they were the only crew getting a late start had everyone on edge. But snow crab season ended up being incredibly lucrative. They'd hit their quota in three days then returned home today. Exhausted yet happy.

Mostly happy, anyway. He could hardly stand being apart from Mia.

He trudged toward the kitchen. Mom had taken care of Poppy while he'd been at sea. She and Poppy were spending the afternoon with Carina. Probably so Poppy could play with her cousins and Carina could stay in bed. The latest text he'd received said they'd be on their way home soon. Normally, he couldn't wait to see his little girl. But for now, he needed a few minutes to gather his thoughts. When he'd gotten off the boat, he'd received a text message from the lab, and an email from the donor registry. He was a viable match for someone in need of stem cells. Mrs. Madden's condition had dominated his thoughts on his drive back to the house. There was no way to know if he was her match.

But now he had a reason to call Mia.

Gus made ice packs from the ice in his freezer, grabbed a drink from the fridge, plus a kitchen towel, and returned to the living room. He dropped onto the couch, sandwiched ice bags on the shoulder that hurt the most, then reached for his phone.

Dredging up his courage, he scrolled to Mia's number and called her.

"Hello?"

"Hey." He tried to sound calm. Pretend that they hadn't shared a tense, emotional goodbye. Thankfully, she couldn't know that his heart was pounding like a freight train in his chest.

"Hi." She sniffed.

Was she crying? "What's wrong?"

"She's beautiful and perfect, and everybody loves her, and I can't even stand it." Her words tumbled out.

"Mia," he said. "Hold on. Back up. What's going on?"

"It's Lexi." Mia's voice wobbled. "She flew in last night. Met the whole family. Well, the family that's here, anyway. Of course, they all adore her. Did I mention she's beautiful and perfect? I've never heard a more adorable accent."

Gus tried not to smile. "I'm sure she's not perfect. We all have our faults."

"Apparently no one here got the memo."

"How long is she going to stay?"

"Get this. She only bought a *one-way* ticket. Watch, next she'll buy a house and live here forever."

"The commemoration is happening soon, right? You've got about a week to go. Maybe she'll head back home after that." Gus shifted his position on the couch, knocking one of his ice bags loose. He slapped it back into place.

"Doubt it. I'm sorry, I'm being very needy right now. Feel free to tell me that I need to grow up."

"I would never tell you that."

Silence filled the line. "Thank you. I don't deserve your kindness."

"Ha. That's cute," he said. "You could vent to me a million times and I'd still be in your debt."

"After the things I said to you before you left, I'm surprised you're still speaking to me."

He scrambled to find the right words to respond. He'd been praying for an opportunity to reconnect. He had felt self-absorbed in that moment, asking God to give him another chance with Mia. But maybe his prayers weren't so misguided after all. All he could do was hope that God would somehow give him the words to encourage Mia.

"Gus? Are you there?"

"Yeah, I'm here. Listen, I get that Lexi's arrival is difficult for you," he said. "There are so many questions, and everyone is so excited to meet her. I'm sure if you asked Lexi, she'd tell you that this is overwhelming for her, too."

"I can't ask her because they're taking her around town to all of Hearts Bay's best locations."

"You're skipping the field trip, right?"

"One hundred percent. I had to make up some dumb excuse, because there was no way I could handle listening while Dad showed her all their favorite spots."

"Wait, isn't she married? Doesn't her husband care about her being gone so long?"

"Her husband's deployed overseas or something. I didn't get all the details."

"I'm sorry that you're having a tough time."

"This is much harder than I thought it was going to be. I'd convinced myself that I could do anything, but I'm not sure I can do this."

"Mia, you don't have to *do* anything."

"But I can't pretend this isn't happening, or that I wasn't switched at birth. The DNA evidence from the online service she used indicates that she's a Madden."

"I—I know." Gus paused. He was teetering on the edge of flubbing this. Did she not see that her loyalty to her family might be causing her pain? He drew a calming breath. This wasn't the time to get aggravated. "All I'm saying is, maybe it's not your job to micromanage this. She's a grown woman. This was her decision to take this step to meet her biological family."

"But she might also be a match for my mom— her mom—ugh. Whatever. You know what I mean."

"Yeah, about that," Gus said. "I have some news to share."

"What is it?"

"I have an update from the lab. I'm a possible match for a patient. What if it's your mom?"

"Gus, we talked about this. Donating is time-consuming and you'll have to travel."

"And someone you love is sick. Why won't you let me help?"

"Because you have enough—"

"I have enough problems already. I'm not trustworthy. Is that what you were going to say?" He plucked the ice bags off his shoulder and tossed them on the floor. So much for not getting aggravated. Man, she was stubborn.

The silence made him wince. His tone hadn't been all that gentle, either.

"Look, I'm worn out. You've had an emotional day. The last thing I want to do is argue with you," he said softly.

"Thank you for your generous offer, but like I said the last time, it's not necessary."

"I can't ignore the results, Mia. Someone needs me to help them get well. I can't live with myself if I don't follow through. If I'm confirmed as a match, I'm going to donate."

"Your generosity is admirable. But no one would fault you for putting your job and your child first."

He pressed his lips together. Poppy came first. Always. But why couldn't he do both? Be a dad and help someone struggling with a health crisis?

"It's been a long day. For both of us. Poppy will be home soon and I need to get dinner started. Keep me posted on how things are going there."

"Thanks for listening," she said. "Have a good night."

Mia ended the call.

Gus released a low growl of irritation then dropped his phone on the cushions beside him. He'd feared this would happen. She refused to accept his help because she didn't trust him. Why did he think that he could swoop in like a superhero and save her from her heartache?

* * *

Everything Mia had said to Gus was true. Lexi was perfect.

Mia was sitting at the table in her parents' kitchen, pushing food around on her plate and counting the minutes until she could leave. Lexi was at the opposite end of the table. She wore a light chambray shirt layered over a navy-and-white striped T-shirt. Her long, dark hair had been blown perfectly straight. Her cheekbones were to die for. Even her eyebrows looked incredible.

Dad cracked a joke and Lexi laughed. It was a lyrical sound that nearly matched Tess's laugh.

Clearly, the family adored her already.

Mia swallowed a bite of enchilada casserole. Her envy made her stomach hurt.

Or maybe that was the shame she carried after pouring her heart out to Gus on the phone. He didn't deserve to be on the receiving end of her wrath. But she had to tell someone. These feelings would eat her alive otherwise. Sure, she was behaving like a jealous, petty schoolgirl. But wouldn't anyone in her situation feel envious?

More laughter erupted around the table. Mia stole a quick glance at Lexi. She seemed right at home here. Not the type of person who needed to hold court or had arrived with a hidden agenda. Her witty sense of humor reminded Mia of Charlie. What would he have to say about all of this?

Mia sipped her water. If she finished her dinner and skipped dessert to help clean up, she'd be able to leave within the hour. Suddenly, she sensed all eyes were on her.

"Mia, did you hear what Lexi asked?" Dad added another dollop of sour cream to his second serving of casserole.

"No. Sorry, I guess I was daydreaming." Mia forced a smile. "What did I miss?"

"You're thinking about that handsome fisherman of yours, aren't you?" Rylee shot her a knowing look. "Busted."

Mia glared. "Let's not talk about Gus tonight."

Rylee winced. "Sorry."

Asher had stayed home with Cameron, who had a project to work on for school. Tess had stopped by with Lucy. She stood behind her parents with the baby asleep in a sling tied to her chest. She swayed back and forth. The disapproving look on her face made Mia squirm.

Mia turned her attention toward Lexi. "Could you please repeat the question?"

"I was wondering how the plans were coming along for the commemoration? Rylee mentioned you're on the planning committee," Lexi said.

"I was on the committee. One member of the

committee felt I wasn't moving quickly enough, so I've stepped down."

"Oh, dear." Mom frowned. "You didn't tell me that."

Mia shrugged. "We've had a lot going on."

Rylee dragged a tortilla chip through a pool of salsa on her plate. "It was Mrs. Lovell who complained, wasn't it?"

"Have you met the other people that were born the same day as us?" Lexi declined the second helping of casserole Dad offered her.

"Most of them live here," Mia said. "Two others live in Anchorage, but last I heard, they were planning to come back for the event."

"I'd love to meet them." Lexi reached for her glass of water. "If there's anything I can do to help, let me know. I love to plan, and I love a good party."

"You're one of the honored guests," Rylee said. "We couldn't ask you to plan the event."

Lexi's brow furrowed. "But Mia said she was part of the planning committee. Isn't she considered one of the honored guests?"

"Like I said, they weren't pleased with my performance, so I had to step aside." Mia stood and carried her plate to the sink. A flurry of group texts from the committee one night after a particularly difficult day at the clinic, high-lighting all the tasks that hadn't been completed yet, had prompted Mia to hastily resign via email. She'd felt a tiny bit guilty, but it was for the best. They'd wanted to meet every week for the whole month of April, which she couldn't do. Two committee members had argued about the kinds of flowers they'd wanted on the table centerpieces. Mia had suggested they skip the flowers because they weren't necessary. She'd also recommended they cancel the order of helium balloons because it might be too windy, and neither suggestion had been well received.

Gus had been right. She should've stepped down after Mrs. Lovell confronted her at the Trading Post. Mia rinsed her plate and added it to the dishwasher, along with her silverware.

"Are you leaving?" Tess asked.

"Don't go yet." Mom held up her hand. "There's something important we need to discuss."

The room fell silent.

Mia returned to the table and sat down in her chair.

"What's going on?" Dad asked.

"A potential donor match has been identified." Mom's voice thickened with unshed tears. "I just received the news a few minutes ago."

"A donor match?" Lexi's gaze flitted around the table. "Does someone need a kidney?"

They hadn't told her. Mia twisted an unused

paper napkin around her fingers. Someone else needed to explain to Lexi that the mother she'd connected with had a serious health condition.

Mom covered Lexi's hand with her own. "I have aplastic anemia."

Lexi turned the bracelets on her wrist in a slow circle. "I don't believe I'm familiar with that. What is it?"

"My bone marrow has failed. It's not producing new, healthy cells, so it's easy for me to get sick." Mom held out her arm. "You might have noticed that I have a lot of bruises, and I struggle with fatigue."

"I had noticed but didn't want to pry."

"This has been going on for a while. Blood transfusions help some. Mia's been working hard to give me the best care possible. Chronic infections are getting worse because standard treatments are not as effective as we hoped."

Dad looped his arm around her shoulders. "That's why a stem-cell transplant from a viable donor could give her immune system the boost that she needs."

"What if it doesn't work?" Lexi asked. "Can the body reject the donation? What happens then?"

Mia glanced at her parents, silently asking permission.

"Tell her," Mom said. "There's no reason for her not to know."

"In more severe cases of aplastic anemia, patients may encounter heart failure."

Lexi gasped. "That's awful."

"We're doing everything we can to make sure that doesn't happen." Mia infused her voice with the calm, confident tone she used when delivering less-than-ideal information to her patients. "I'm thrilled to hear you have a potential donor match, Mom. Hopefully, the transplant will happen in Anchorage as soon as the healthy cells have been harvested from the donor. Sometimes the patient does chemo or radiation first, if the doctor feels that's the best treatment plan. Assuming Mom's body will tolerate the procedure."

Lexi's eyes gleamed with unshed tears. "Your body will tolerate the procedure. I know it will. And if you find out you need another donor, I'm happy to get tested too."

"Thank you, sweetheart." Mom leaned over and kissed Lexi's cheek. "We're so glad you're here."

Mia looked away. Her conversation with Gus infiltrated her thoughts. Was he the potential match for her mother? That hardly seemed possible. The timing could just be a coincidence. She pushed back her chair, stood and carried the casserole pan to the sink. She didn't want to think about Gus right now.

Lexi's positive attitude was admirable. But she hadn't been here for the grueling months of fevers, recurring infections and endless hours of internet research. She had no idea how challenging this had been for their family. Terrifying, really.

Lexi hasn't had an easy time, either.

Mia rummaged in the cabinet for a container to hold the leftovers. Dad had mentioned that Lexi's family wasn't happy that she'd connected with the Maddens. No one had spelled it out, but Mia sensed they weren't eager to hear more about her.

Hot tears pricked her eyes. She refused to cry. Not here. Because then she'd have to explain herself and she wasn't about to admit that Lexi's arrival had stirred up feelings of jealousy and abandonment.

How could she feel abandoned by people she'd never met and hadn't known existed?

Three days after getting the news that he was a potential donor match, Gus had packed his bag and booked a flight to Anchorage. He'd asked his neighbor to drive him to Dillingham's airport. If Liesel would come by and pick up Poppy like they'd planned he'd be all set.

The coordinator at the outpatient facility had sent him a text with a link for tomorrow's check-in instructions. His procedure to donate stem cells required five consecutive days of injections to stimulate blood stem cell growth. On the fifth day, his blood stem cells would be harvested from his blood in a lengthy procedure. If all went well, the coordinator assured him he'd be finished after one session. If they didn't need an additional donation, he'd be able to fly home the following day.

However, a terrible storm had blown in this morning, pummeling Dillingham with high winds. Through the living-room window, he could barely see the outline of the houses across the road. Heavy snow blew sideways. Thick gray clouds dipped low. The possibility of a plane landing or taking off in this mess seemed bleak.

Gus sat on the couch with Poppy nestled in his lap. He stared at the weather forecast on television, hoping it might offer better news soon. Poppy leaned against him. The heat radiating off her little body prompted a fresh wave of concern.

He pressed his palm to her forehead. "You're really warm, sweet girl."

She glanced up at him, her thumb wedged in her mouth. Flushed cheeks and a glassy-eyed stare propelled him into action.

"Let's check your temperature." He tried to

ease her off his lap and onto the couch. She whined and clung to him. "I'm sorry you don't feel well. Don't worry. I'm going to help you." He gently scooped her into his arms then carried her to the kitchen and set her on the floor by his feet. Thankfully, she was distracted by letter-shaped magnets on the fridge. He poured apple juice in a sippy cup, grabbed a package of crackers from the cabinet, then found his phone on the counter.

No updates from Liesel.

Her last text had said she was snowed in. Planes weren't flying out of Kotzebue, either.

Super. Grounded planes, no Liesel and a kid who didn't feel well. He handed Poppy her sippy cup. She eyed it suspiciously but took it.

If he missed his appointment in Anchorage, his donation would be delayed. Whoever needed his healthy stem cells would be stuck waiting even longer. What if it was Mrs. Madden? He'd signed the appropriate paperwork to have his donor-contact information shared with the patient. It didn't seem likely that he'd know if he was a match for Mrs. Madden, though. If Mia knew, she hadn't shared the details with him. He'd texted her his flight info and told her he'd scheduled the procedure.

She'd acknowledged the text and shared the name of the hotel where she and her family were staying. Mrs. Madden had been admitted to the hospital in Anchorage. He'd quickly written back and asked to see her. She'd agreed to meet him in the hotel lobby at six-thirty tonight.

Ever since their emotional goodbye in the Maddens' driveway, he hadn't stopped thinking about Mia. About a future together. Being back on the water on board the *Zafiro* had been demanding. A couple of times he'd wanted to vomit over the side, and handling the crab pots had been brutal, but he'd found quiet moments. To pray. To thank God for His provision. And to plead for yet another opportunity to have a relationship with Mia.

Poppy pushed her sippy cup into his leg. "Yuck."

"Poppy, you have to drink something."

She shook her head and set the cup on the floor.

He sighed and ripped open the package of crackers.

"Mine?" She held up her hand, pointing.

"Yes, these are for you. Here." He handed her one. She snatched it and nibbled on the corner.

Oh, boy. It was shaping up to be a rough evening. "We need to check your temperature."

She held the cracker in one hand and rearranged the magnets on the fridge with the other. He walked down the hall to the bathroom and found his thermometer in the drawer. A quick search of his shaving kit produced a bottle of medication for infants and toddlers. Liesel had sent it with Dean when he'd brought Poppy to Hearts Bay. Gus double-checked the label to make sure it was meant for reducing fevers. He shook the bottle. Hopefully, he had enough to give her a dose.

Back in the kitchen, Poppy spotted the medicine and burst into tears.

"Shhhh, it's okay, pumpkin. Let's see if you have a fever." Gus sat beside her on the floor and quickly checked her temperature with the ear thermometer. The number 100.7 appeared on the digital screen. Poppy pooched out her lower lip. Her little body trembled as she tried to stop crying.

He set down the thermometer, dosed the medicine and somehow convinced Poppy to take it. She swallowed, made a terrible face, then pushed his hand away.

"Good girl." Gus handed her the apple juice again. "Try this."

She took a small sip then gave him the cup back.

Poppy stood then toddled over to the kitchen table. She'd left one of her baby dolls buckled into an umbrella stroller parked beside the chairs. While she pushed the stroller back to-

ward the living room, Gus retrieved his phone.
Liesel wasn't coming home tonight. He wasn't
going to make his flight to Anchorage. There
was nothing else he could do except send Mia
an update. Then pray that the skies cleared by
morning. Because despite the obstacles keeping them apart, he wasn't giving up. He'd told
Mia he'd see her soon and he fully intended to
keep his word.

Gus should've been here by now. Where was
he?

Mia paced the hotel lobby, the carpet slick
against the soles of her ballet flats. She stopped
and glanced out the wide windows facing the
busy street. Cars, trucks and taxis cruised by.
People on the sidewalks wore knit hats and winter jackets. Their breath escaped in puffs of
white as they walked. In the distance, snow-cov-
ered mountains framed the city of Anchorage.
The afternoon sun, making its final appearance for the day as it slid toward the horizon,
painted the tops and sides of buildings in gorgeous shades of lavender and pink.

Mom had already been admitted to the hospital. Dad and the rest of her family waited patiently in the lobby. They'd planned to grab a
quick dinner at a nearby restaurant. Mia had
asked them to wait a few minutes so she could

see Gus. She'd been ridiculously excited all day, checking the time at least once an hour, willing it to be six-thirty.

Except it was almost seven and he hadn't shown up.

She rubbed her hand against the ache in her chest. What if he wasn't coming? What if there weren't any other potential donors for her mother? A stem-cell transplant was the only cure for aplastic anemia. Yes, okay, there was a slim possibility that Lexi might be a match. She'd already had her cheek swabbed and they were waiting for the results.

But Mom wasn't doing well, and Gus had been the proverbial light at the end of a very dark tunnel. Usually a donor and patient's contact information were kept confidential, but the person who'd handed her the paperwork at the intake desk had accidentally disclosed Gus's identity.

Her phone hummed with an incoming text.

I'm weathered in. Liesel is stuck in Kotzebue because her plane is grounded, too. Looks like I can't get out for another day, maybe two. I'll keep you posted.

Hot tears blurred her vision as she stared at Gus's message.

He wasn't coming.

She'd known this. Deep in her core, she'd carried the ominous feeling that Gus would let her down. That's who he was. A man who couldn't keep his promises.

He'd insisted he'd changed. That he would never do anything to hurt her. She'd been an idiot to think this time would be different.

Another text pinged. How is your mom doing? I've left a message with my coordinator asking to reschedule ASAP.

She choked back a sob. Seriously?

Mom is not doing well. I can't believe you're not coming. We can't afford to wait for you to reschedule.

She sent the text then jammed her phone in the back pocket of her jeans. Drawing her cardigan tighter around her, she stared out the window. How was she supposed to tell her family that their donor match was a no-show?

Her phone rang. She swiped at the tears on her cheeks with her fingertips then retrieved her phone.

Gus's name and number filled the screen.

Nope. She declined the call and put her phone away. There was no way she could speak to him right now. He'd deserted her and her family at the worst possible time.

It rang again, and this time she ignored it.

"Mia?"

Rylee joined her at the window and pressed her hand to Mia's shoulder. "Everything okay?"

Mia sniffed. "Gus isn't coming."

"Oh, no."

"I can't believe this is happening." Mia shook her head. "We planned for every possibility."

"Except the weather." Rylee rubbed Mia's back. "That's a nasty storm in western Alaska. Planes can't get in or out."

"Gus should've planned for that," Mia blurted. "He should have flown in sooner to dodge the storm."

Confusion filled Rylee's eyes. "That's a lot to ask of someone who committed to spending five days undergoing a procedure to donate stem cells. He has a child and responsibilities. This isn't Gus's fault."

Mia clamped her lips tight.

"Wait. You're blaming him. Mia, that's not right."

Mia sniffed again, then dug in the pocket of her sweater for a tissue. "I knew it was a long shot, but a small part of me truly believed he could make this happen. But to be honest I've never been able to trust him. Now he's let me down at the most crucial time. I can't… I'm really angry."

"I understand how much you wanted this to work. There are so many factors here that we can't control. The fact that Gus even wanted to try to help is amazing. Right?"

"Please don't defend him right now."

Rylee's eyes widened. "I'm not going to let you hold this against him. He didn't do anything wrong. I don't understand why you can't appreciate what a wonderful—"

"Rylee, please." Mia held up her hand to interrupt. "I can't talk about this anymore. You guys go on to dinner without me. I'm not hungry."

"But Dad wanted us to eat together. We've been waiting for you for thirty minutes."

"I'll order room service or something later. Go ahead without me."

She brushed past Rylee and hurried toward the elevator. A fresh wave of tears clogged her throat. The procedure wasn't going to happen tomorrow. Not only had Gus let her down, but she'd also failed at helping the woman she'd always known as her mother get well.

Chapter Thirteen

Gus sat at his kitchen table, coffee in one hand and his phone in the other. A text message from his captain filled the bubble on his screen.

Thinking about expanding the fleet and putting a boat in Hearts Bay for next crab season. Are you in?

Gus released a frustrated groan and let his phone clatter to the table. An intriguing message, but it was too little, too late. Sure, getting a position on a crew for next season sounded like a fantastic opportunity. But why move to Hearts Bay if he didn't have Mia in his life?

Besides, sending Poppy back and forth between Hearts Bay and Dillingham was out of the question. There was no way he'd put his daughter through that, even if Liesel agreed to it.

Down the hall in the bathroom, the shower turned on. Dean was singing a popular country song off-key. Gus shook his head then stood to pour a second cup of coffee. He'd loved having his brother around again, but he wouldn't miss the terrible shower singing when Dean went back to Montana next week.

In the living room, Poppy was still in her pajamas. She stood at the coffee table with a bowl of dry Cheerios in front of her and a kids' show from the PBS channel playing on TV. Her fever was gone. The storm had passed, planes were flying again and he expected Liesel to come and pick up Poppy soon.

He added cream and a heaping spoonful of sugar to his coffee. A boat based in Hearts Bay. Yeah, he'd dismissed the notion almost as quickly as he read the message. Doubt niggled at him. What if he said yes? What if God had orchestrated circumstances to put him back near Mia?

A knock at the front door tugged him from his thoughts. Leaving his mug on the counter, he padded into the entryway.

"Who that, Daddy?" Poppy gobbled another handful of dry cereal.

"I don't know, pumpkin. Let's see." He opened the door.

"Hi." Liesel offered a tight smile, then brushed past him and stepped inside uninvited.

"Sure, come on in."

Poppy's whole face lit up. "Mommy!"

Liesel ignored Gus and sank to her knees on the carpet. "How's my baby girl?"

Poppy knocked over her cereal and raced into Liesel's outstretched arms.

Gus closed the door behind her. Liesel scooped up Poppy and swung her around, planting a noisy kiss on her cheek. "I missed you so much."

Poppy giggled and grabbed two fists of Liesel's long blond hair. "Mommy, I flied."

"I know, I heard. Lots of airplane rides for my girl. You're getting so big. Was it fun?"

Poppy's smile faded. "Miss Mia."

Oh, boy. Her honesty slugged him. *Not great timing, pumpkin.*

Liesel let Poppy slide to the floor. "Why don't you watch your show while I talk to your dad for a minute?"

Poppy obeyed. Liesel faced him, her expression a neutral mask he couldn't decipher. He was in no mood to argue.

"Gus, I—"

"Mia isn't anyone to be concerned about." He'd go ahead and put a stop to the inquisition before it even started. "We're not together."

"I'm not here to talk to you about your girlfriend." Liesel shrugged out of her jacket and hung it on the rack beside the door. "I do want to talk to you about Hearts Bay, though, because this isn't working."

His scalp prickled. "What's not working?"

She heaved a sigh. "I know I probably should have said something before now but there's a position open in Hearts Bay. At the police department. I applied and I've already passed the initial phone screening."

Yeah, he definitely was going to need that second cup of coffee. "Would you like some coffee? Sounds like this could be a long conversation."

"Please."

He led the way into the kitchen. "Have a seat."

Liesel sat down at the table. He poured her cup, grabbed his own refilled mug and carried them both to the table. "Did your assignment not go well? What was all that talk about getting a promotion if you did what they asked you to do?"

"Thank you for the coffee." Liesel scooted the mug closer. A tendril of steam curled in the air. "The position here was already offered to someone else."

"Oh. I'm sorry to hear that." Gus took a sip of his coffee.

"My efforts weren't appreciated. There's not going to be a lot of upward mobility here. I saw the position in Hearts Bay and wanted to ask you about relocating. They clearly have a robust fishing fleet."

Gus dragged his hand through his hair. "That's a huge move, Liesel. If we both go and you decide you don't like it, or the job doesn't work out, or the chief doesn't promote you, I'm not willing to move again to accommodate your next job change. Are we clear?"

Liesel sat back in her chair. The muscles in her throat tightened as she swallowed. "That's fair."

"Is it?"

He couldn't hide his skepticism. They'd been down this path on more than one occasion. He'd agree to her plans, then she'd change her mind at the last minute and upend everything, then conveniently blame him instead of accepting responsibility for a poor decision.

"I understand your concerns. I'm sure this sounds flighty and impulsive, but this opportunity is promising. If you don't mind my asking, are you seeing someone who lives there?"

He blew out an impatient sigh. "It's complicated."

"I know I haven't exactly been your biggest cheerleader, but—"

His laughter lacked humor. "That's an understatement."

She pinned him with a pleading look. "Come on, Gus. I'm trying here."

"All right. I'm listening." He sipped his coffee and dismissed the barbed comments piling up in his head.

"You have every right to be suspicious and doubtful of my intentions. At the end of the day, I truly want you to be happy. I want us to do what's best for Poppy."

He almost choked on his coffee. What could he possibly say to that? For once he and Liesel were on the same page. It had to be a God thing. "I'm open to moving to Hearts Bay if you get the job."

"Great. I'll keep you updated." She pulled her phone from her pocket. "Can we review our arrangements for the next couple of weeks? I owe you big-time for taking Poppy while I was away."

"In that case, I'm going to need a favor." He picked up his phone. Mia was upset with him for missing his flight and his donation procedure. Now he wanted to make things right. Liesel's unexpected kindness had paved the way for him to keep his word.

"Please, please hurry." Alone in the hospital elevator, Mia shifted from one foot to the other, willing the car to rise faster. She'd overslept. About thirty minutes ago, a series of text messages woke her up. Horrified, she realized she'd turned off her alarm and missed multiple calls from Rylee, Tess and their father.

Mom's condition had deteriorated drastically overnight. Dad had summoned the family to her bedside. Sick with worry, Mia had thrown on the same clothes she'd discarded the night before then caught a cab to the hospital.

The elevator eased to a stop on the fifth floor. When the doors parted, Mia barreled into the corridor. Through the broad expanse of windows, dismal gray skies blocked any view of the mountains. The storm that had blanketed western Alaska and grounded flights must've set Anchorage in its sights.

Her flats squeaked on the linoleum as she jogged toward Mom's room at the far end of the fifth floor. Rylee's most recent text had urged her to come quickly. Terror clawed at her insides. Then the familiar timbre of her father's voice slowed her steps. She rounded the corner. A small alcove with a sitting area, water fountain and restrooms separated the hallway from the rest of the fifth floor.

Two men wearing teal scrubs under white coats sat in beige club chairs. A nondescript coffee table with a faux floral centerpiece divided them from Mia's family members. Dad stood beside the sofa, his feet in a wide stance and his arms crossed over his plaid shirt. Beside him on the beige sofa, Rylee, Tess and Lexi sat crammed together holding hands.

When did Lexi get here? There was no room for Mia to sit. Those thoughts slammed together in her head, sending both surprise and jealousy cascading through her.

"I'm so sorry I'm late." Her chest heaved as she tried to catch her breath. "What did I miss?"

The physicians glanced at her father. She recognized one as the attending physician, and the other must have come on shift this morning. Their not-so-subtle request for permission to continue the discussion rankled.

"This is Mia, our oldest daughter," Dad said. "She's a physician assistant in Hearts Bay."

Satisfied she was worthy of receiving their information, both men shifted in their seats. "We were sharing with your family that Mrs. Madden's condition is concerning. Oxygen levels have dropped. Based on her latest CBC, her blood cell counts are dangerously low. Our recommendation is that she leave for Seattle as soon as possible. A stem-cell transplant is no longer a viable option here."

Mia's breath hitched. Seattle?

"There are two seats on the afternoon flight."

Rylee held up her phone. "I can buy your tickets right now."

"Hold on." Mia shrugged out of her jacket. A cold sweat made her shirt stick to her back. "If her condition has deteriorated, are you confident she can handle a transfer? I thought a stem-cell transplant was the only effective treatment plan."

An awkward silence blanketed the sitting area. The attending physician's mouth was set at an unforgiving angle.

Dad shifted his weight. "The team here feels she'll benefit from being under the care of Dr. Westheimer."

"Who is…?" Mia scrutinized the men sitting before her. They were likely well-regarded in the medical community. She was pushing the professional boundaries by challenging them, but this was her *mother*.

"Dr. Westheimer is a leading expert in treating aplastic anemia. Particularly the more complicated cases. A potential donor in the Seattle area has been identified whose markers are a closer match for Mrs. Madden." The doctor seated closest to Mia cleared his throat. "Mrs. Madden meets the criteria for complicated."

She'd always hated that word when it referenced a patient's status. It meant they'd exhausted all their options and didn't have a viable next step in their protocol. "Isn't she susceptible to infection? All that recirculated air on the plane?"

"If you'd prefer to hire a private plane staffed with a physician and nurse to transfer your mother, you are more than welcome to do so." The younger physician crossed one leg over the other. "My recommendation remains the same. Timing is everything here. If you secure seats on this afternoon's flight, your mother can consult with Dr. Westheimer this evening, or first thing tomorrow."

"She's received a full course of antibiotics through her IV. Time is of the essence," the attending physician added. "Dr. Westheimer will provide excellent care."

Mia sank onto the arm of the sofa. This couldn't be happening. Why didn't they call their sooner? *How* had she overslept?

A woman's voice on the overhead speaker summoned one of the doctors by name. He stood and shook her father's hand. "Pleasure to meet you, Mr. Madden. My team will get you the necessary paperwork. As soon as you have confirmation for your flight, you can be on your way."

Dad shook both doctors' hands. "Thank you."

The men offered everyone else curt nods, then strode down the hall and disappeared behind another set of double doors.

Mia buried her face in her hands.

"Mia, it's okay. This is good news." Rylee squeezed her leg. "Mom's going to get the best possible care available."

"You don't know that." Mia dropped her hands in her lap, then stood and paced the alcove. "I was getting her the best care that she needed. At least I thought I was. I shouldn't have kept her in Hearts Bay. We stayed on the island way too long. Dad, did you talk to anybody else? Get another opinion? Do you know anything about this Westen…whatever? I mean, maybe he's a leading expert, but I've never heard of him. How do we know—"

"Mia, honey." Dad stepped into her path and held up his palms. "Take a deep breath. It's all going to be okay. You have done everything that you possibly know how to do. No one expected you to cure her."

"I did." Mia's voice broke. "I expected me to fix this. What have I done? What if it's too late?" She fell into her father's arms, sobbing.

Later that day, Mia sat slumped in a chair at a gate in the Anchorage airport. Lexi sat beside her, flipping through a fashion magazine. Rylee sat across from her, sipping the last of her soft drink. They'd just finished eating at the airport's food court.

Their parents had already left for Seattle. Mia's throat was raw and her eyes felt scratchy from crying so much.

She just wanted to go home.

Outside, bright lights near the end of the jetway illuminated the heavy snow falling from the night sky. Mia checked the screen mounted behind the agent standing at the counter nearby. Their flight to Hearts Bay had been pushed back an hour.

She tucked her hands inside the pockets of her puffy jacket and tried to ignore Rylee's pointed stare. Finally, Mia couldn't take it anymore. She leveled Rylee with what she hoped was a piercing gaze.

"Something on your mind, Rylee?"

Rylee rattled the ice in her disposable cup. She'd crossed one leg over the other and now her foot bobbed in the air. "Heard from Gus today?"

"Nope."

"Would you answer if he called or sent a text?"

"Nope."

Rylee rolled her eyes. "Why are you being so hard on him? The guy's been relentless in his pursuit of you and all you've done is push him away."

Ouch. Mia couldn't argue with that last part. She'd most definitely pushed Gus away. "We've talked about this already. Losing Abner and

Charlie did a number on me. I don't want to love another fisherman."

Lexi reached out and patted Mia's arm. "I don't blame you for being scared. It's hard to put ourselves out there."

"Not helping, Lexi." Rylee gently nudged Lexi's foot with her own. "You must've been brave at some point because you got married to a man who serves in the military. And you weren't afraid to come here and meet all of us."

"Are you kidding? I was terrified to walk down that aisle and marry Beau. Reaching out to y'all then traveling to Alaska alone scared me to death." Lexi flipped her magazine closed then tucked it into her carry-on. "But the thing is, in both scenarios, the blessings far outweighed the scary parts."

Rylee's gaze swung back to Mia. "Sound advice, don't you think?"

"I've spent the last four years convincing myself that I was better off alone. Afraid to hope that I could love again." Mia fiddled with the zipper on her jacket. "I'm starting to wonder if the Lord brought Gus back into my life to show me that I couldn't have been more wrong. Maybe Gus is exactly what I need."

Rylee squealed then set her cup aside and clapped her hands. "You have no idea how long I've been praying that you'd come to your senses. So you'll call him?"

"Let's not go that far." Mia shifted in her seat. "If Mom's condition improves and we get through the commemoration, maybe I'll reach out."

Rylee didn't even try to hide her disappointment. Mia didn't have it in her to keep rehashing the conversation. The last few days had depleted her emotionally and physically.

Rylee's comments stuck with her though. Gus had been relentless. In the best possible way. But doubt still lingered. Was he truly part of God's plan for her life?

Chapter Fourteen

He had to get to the commemoration. Gus stood outside the airport in Hearts Bay, his duffel bag on the ground at his feet. His connecting flight in Anchorage had been delayed and now he had less than twenty minutes to get into town. Rylee had texted him that Mia, Lexi and the others would be recognized during a brief ceremony at 1:30 p.m. He surveyed the parking lot. There wasn't a single cab available. Flowers in the planters flanking the doors danced in the breeze. The May weather hinted at spring. Sunlight pierced mottled clouds overhead. Thankfully, the forecasted rain had held off.

Now if he could just find a ride.

Maybe he should've called ahead and asked a friend to pick him up. Everyone who came to mind was probably already at the event. The automatic doors whooshed open behind him. He turned. A woman who looked familiar walked outside. She carried several sleeves of disposable paper cups and plastic lids in her arms. Two sleeves slid from her grasp and landed on the ground.

"Need some help?" Gus picked up the plastic-wrapped cups.

"Please." She gave him a friendly once-over. Recognition flashed in her eyes. "Aren't you Mia's friend? The guy who survived the accident on the *Imogene*?"

"I'm Gus Coleman." He held onto the sleeves of cups. The bundle she was clutching in her arms didn't look stable enough to add more.

"Nice to see you again. I'm Annie. I run the coffee shop."

"That's right. You're good friends with the Maddens."

"Sure am." She grinned. "Need a ride into town?"

"How'd you guess?"

"Oh, just a hunch." She angled her head toward the parking lot. "C'mon, I'll drop you off on Main Street. My Jeep's over here."

"Great. Thank you." He tucked the cups under one arm and grabbed his duffel bag with his other hand. "I'm surprised you're not at the commemoration, too."

"I was running low on cups and lids. We had

to overnight more from Anchorage. They came in on your flight."

Gus followed her to a black Jeep, then helped her load the cups, lids and his bag.

He climbed into the passenger seat. Annie circled around and slid behind the wheel.

"You've been away for a few months right?"

He buckled his seat belt. "Not because I wanted to be."

Annie studied him, then turned the key in the ignition. "Does Mia know you're back?"

"No."

Annie's mouth tightened.

Uh-oh. He clutched the overhead handle mounted near the doorframe. "Is there something I should know?"

She hesitated, then checked behind her before backing out of the parking space. "You're going to find out eventually, I suppose. Mrs. Madden isn't doing well. She's been in the hospital in Seattle for the last six days. Mia plans to leave tonight to be with her."

Gus's mouth went dry. "That's not good. Did she ever get her stem-cell transplant?"

"No. The doctors in Anchorage recommended she transfer to Seattle so a specialist could care for her. She hasn't been stable enough for another procedure. We're all super worried." Annie drove out of the airport parking lot and eased onto the highway leading to Hearts Bay. The blue-green water lapped against the rocky shoreline. On the opposite side of the road, a dense forest of green trees stood like an army marching toward the base of a mountain. In the distance, sunlight reflected off the rigging on a fishing boat. The beauty of Hearts Bay was breathtaking. Hard to believe he'd insisted on leaving such a gorgeous island. Until he'd spent time with Mia and her family. Now thoughts of buying a house, getting a job on a boat based here and someday sending Poppy to one of the local elementary schools spooled through his head.

Except none of those plans were a possibility if Liesel didn't get the job she'd applied for here. Or if Mia refused to speak to him. They hadn't spoken or exchanged any text messages since he'd told her the storm in Dillingham had kept him grounded. Doubt sloshed in, like an icy wave cresting over the bow of his vessel. Maybe showing up unannounced was a terrible idea. Annie graciously kept him distracted while she drove. They chatted about the coffee business, her favorite childhood memories from growing up on Orca Island and all the ways the heart-shaped rocks had drawn engaged couples to the area for their weddings.

A few minutes later, Annie pulled into a parking space behind the Trading Post. Gus swiped his clammy palms on his jeans then climbed out of the Jeep.

"If you walk around to the front of the building, the commemoration is over at the community park. Follow the noise and look for the white tent." Annie patted his shoulder. "Hope I didn't freak you out. I'm sure Mia will be glad to see you."

"I hate to ask, but could I buy Mia's favorite drink? She loves your chai lattes."

"That she does." Annie opened the back door and piled sleeves of cups in his arms. "Carry these in for me and that drink will be on the house."

"Deal."

"You're a sweet guy, Gus." Annie led the way toward the back entrance to her shop.

He followed her inside. The aroma of coffee welcomed him. "I'm trying to be a better human."

"Well, that's what we like to hear." Annie showed him where to stack the cups. Then she scooted behind the counter and quickly added cups and lids to the meager supply beside the espresso machine. "I'll make her latte. You can leave your bag in the storage room if you don't want to carry it."

"Thank you. I'll grab the rest of the cups and lids."

After Gus had stowed the rest of the cups, lids and his duffel bag in the back storage room, he stood near the register, hands tucked in his jacket pockets, and surveyed the shop. Only one customer sat at a nearby table. The young girl working for Annie methodically squirted cleaner onto the glass bakery case, then wiped the surface with a cloth. She and Annie chatted over the rumble of the espresso machine.

"Here you go." Annie slipped a cardboard sleeve onto the cup then handed it over. "Enjoy the commemoration."

"Thanks again." He dropped a few bucks in the tip jar.

Annie waved him off. "That is not necessary."

"Whatever. I wouldn't have made it here if not for you."

"Keep me posted," Annie called after him as he strode toward the front door.

Mia's drink in hand, Gus worked his way down the sidewalk, weaving between people strolling outside the shops on Main Street. The top of a white tent in the distance served as his destination. Not that he needed any help locating the event. Annie was right. He just had to follow the noise.

When he reached the edge of the park, the aroma of chili wafted toward him. A team of men and women wearing blue aprons over their jeans and sweatshirts manned the huge vats of soup to his right. Bouquets of flowers dotted the tables filled with chips, salads, fruit and two huge sheet cakes.

Kids darted across the grass, squealing as they chased each other with swords made from balloons. The play structure was swarming with more kids. Gus spotted Cameron, Tess and Asher's boy, zipping down the slide. He was clutching a red balloon sword in his hand. When he landed on the ground at the bottom of the slide, he let out a victorious whoop and punched the air with his balloon sword. Gus couldn't stop a smile.

Everywhere he looked, people milled about, chatting. The round tables and metal folding chairs arranged across the park were filled with more people eating lunch. Alaskans were good at commemorating special events. But he'd never been to a party that commemorated a natural disaster. His chest tightened. He had to find Mia.

A man's voice filtered through the large speakers mounted on either side of the stage. Gus tracked the people lining up on the platform beside the man holding the microphone. When his gaze landed on Mia standing at the far end of the line, his pulse sped. She had styled her auburn hair in bouncy curls. She had on a black leather jacket with lots of zippers, dark washed jeans and short black boots. He liked the edgy look. Warmth bloomed through his chest. He liked it a lot.

Beside Mia, a petite woman who resembled Rylee and Tess stood with her hands clasped in front of her. She was wearing jeans tucked into knee-high brown boots and a red sweater. That had to be Lexi. She smiled like she was enjoying herself.

Gus tried to focus as the man at the podium briefly mentioned each of the eight people celebrating birthdays today, where they lived and what they did for work. Gus grew impatient as the man kept talking. Finally, the honored guests were dismissed and given a round of applause.

Gus couldn't look away as Mia descended the steps. He stood apart from the crowd, holding the cup from the Trading Post. If she saw him, she didn't make eye contact. Disappointment morphed into longing as the crowd swallowed her, blocking his view.

He rarely used his size to his advantage these days, but he couldn't wait another minute to speak with her. Clutching the cup with both hands, he shouldered his way through the people surrounding Lexi, Mia and the others.

When she spotted him over the shoulder of

the woman she was talking to, her eyes widened and her lips parted.

Adrenaline surged through his veins. The woman kept talking, gesturing wildly with her hands. Gus glared at the back of her silver-haired head, willing her to take a breath.

Mia wrapped up the conversation with a pleasant smile and a gentle arm squeeze. Then she slipped past her and stood in front of him. Her gaze collided with his. He braced for harsh words. More rejection. Instead, her fingers trembled as she tucked her hands in her back pockets.

"Gus, hi." Her voice was breathy, hesitant. "What are you doing here?"

He held out the cup. "Happy birthday, Mia."

She reached for the drink. Her beautiful mouth formed a smile. "Thank you."

The air crackled with tension. Awareness. His arms ached to hold her. There was so much he needed to say. "I told you I'd come back, and I'm a man who keeps his promises."

I told you I'd come back.

Something inside her broke free, like an iceberg calving from a glacier. Today was supposed to be about her birth and the natural disaster that had shaped her arrival in the world. But now she realized today was also about freedom. Gus had resurfaced at a time when she'd almost given up on love. She'd struggled with trusting him. But what if he offered her a lifeline?

She'd clung stubbornly to her past with Abner, been so determined to be content with her memories. Standing here, staring at Gus, she allowed herself to consider the possibility that he might be her future. If he'd ever forgive her for the rude things she'd written in that text when he'd missed his flight to Anchorage. She held the cup with both hands, drawing from its warmth. A tremor wracked her body.

Gus was here. Handing her a chai latte, wishing her happy birthday and staring at her with those gorgeous eyes like she was the only woman, the only person, at the commemoration. Voices filtered around her and she sensed the curious stares of onlookers.

Their surroundings faded into the background. She gathered her courage and silently offered a prayer that God would give her the words she needed to pour out her heart to this man.

"Gus, I am so very sorry," she said.

Tenderness filled his eyes. "You don't owe me an apology."

"Oh, but I do."

"I'm the one who insisted that I'd show up for you. Except I've blown it so many times." Anguish twisted his features. "You'll never know how much I regret missing that flight."

"You'll never know how much I regret blaming you for circumstances that aren't ours to control."

His lips parted.

"I know, right? It's hard to believe those words came from my mouth. Rylee helped me understand that I'm a bit of a control freak."

A corner of his mouth twitched. "Really."

"Really." She didn't know where to put her hands, other than on him. Slowly, she walked closer. Gus was a magnet, drawing her in. "Even though I tried to shut her down at the time, she also helped me understand something else. Something very important."

His eyes roamed her face. "What's that?"

"You've been relentless in your pursuit of me."

"Have I?"

"Yes. You have." Emotion tightened her throat. "I kept pushing you away because I was too afraid to let you love me."

"Are you still afraid?"

"A little. Okay, maybe a lot." She quickly set her drink on the ground, then straightened and placed both palms on his broad chest. "But I don't want fear to get in the way anymore."

His brow furrowed. "But what about your mom? Annie told me she's not doing well."

"She's been admitted to the hospital in Seattle. There's a specialist there who's the leading expert in treating aplastic anemia. He identified a donor with more compatible markers. The transplant is scheduled for the day after tomorrow. We're praying that it will be effective and Mom will finally be well."

"I'm sorry I couldn't be there for you in Anchorage. I wanted to be a donor. I still want to be a donor. The coordinator at the facility had me reschedule for next week."

Oh, sweet Gus. Her heart lifted at his passionate concern. She slid her hands across the fabric of his pale blue sweater, then twined them behind his neck. "You're a good man, Gus Coleman. Someone will hopefully have their health restored thanks to your selfless gift."

"People have stepped up for me in my darkest hours. I want to pay that forward." His hands slid under the hem of her jacket and bracketed her waist. "Are you leaving for Seattle today?"

She stroked the short hair at the nape of his neck. He moved closer, his eyes sharp as glass. "I'm flying out tonight. I'll be in Seattle early tomorrow morning."

The wind picked up, blowing thick strands of her hair across her face. Gus's strong fingers tucked the errant curls behind her ear. A rush of goose bumps danced along her skin.

He lowered his hands and gently clasped her upper arms. Why wasn't he saying anything?

His mouth compressed into flat-lipped silence.

Oh, no. Her stomach plunged. Had she completely misread him? "What's wrong?"

"I won't stand between you and your family. If you need to be in Seattle, then I want you to go. If you've made plans to visit your biological family, you need to follow through."

"You're not standing between me and anything. I'll come back from Seattle as soon as I can. I'm choosing *you*, Gus. I want to be with you. It's time for me to release control because I never had it to begin with."

"Are you going to ask me to stop fishing?"

"No."

"Huge swaths of my life are unpredictable, Mia. I have a child and a custody arrangement. Can you honestly say that you're choosing Poppy, too?"

Without hesitation, she drove her chin up. "Absolutely."

"You're already aware that I come with a boatload of emotional baggage. I'm working on forgiving my father, but I don't know if we'll ever mend our broken relationship. I'm an imperfect man, who's made a lot of mistakes."

"Listen to me." She cupped his face with both hands. "While we were apart, the Lord showed me some things that I'd been trying very hard to ignore."

"What's that?"

"I need you. Your strength. Your courage. Your willingness to get back up and try again." Her voice broke. She smiled through the mist of fresh tears. "You've made me want to open my heart again."

The tension in his neck and shoulders eased. Affection stirred in his eyes. "I need you, too. Now I need to say something important."

"I'm listening."

"I love you, Mia."

"I love you, too," she whispered.

"Ever since you saved my life, I've been in awe of you."

She angled her head to one side. "Is that right?"

"You're beautiful, intelligent and I've never known anyone more devoted to the people she loves than you."

"I promise I'll be devoted to you for as long as you'll have me."

"How does forever sound?"

"It sounds perfect."

Then he tunneled his hands into her hair and kissed her. A slow, lingering kiss that drew a smattering of applause and appreciative sighs. Mia lost herself in his embrace and returned the kiss. Gus Coleman was indeed a man who kept his promises.

Epilogue

❧

"One more picture and we'll be all set." Lexi held her finger in the air. "Tip your chin up for me. A smidge more. Now tilt your head. Perfect. Think about Gus and give me your best smile."

Mia's pulse sped in anticipation of seeing Gus at the altar. Her mouth stretched wide. The hairstylist had tamed her hair into a sleek French twist. A slight June breeze rustled the trees nearby and lifted the gauzy fabric of her veil.

Wow, she felt like royalty, posing for her final pictures before she walked down the aisle.

Lexi's magnificent camera clicked and whirred in quick succession. "Oh, my. You are a stunning bride, Mia. I can't wait to see Gus's expression when he puts his eyes on you."

Mia's legs trembled. It wouldn't be long now.

Just over a year had passed since they'd stood at the commemoration and declared their love for one another. She clutched the tissue wrapped around her bouquet. Tears of joy pressed in, but she battled them back.

Lexi lowered the camera, letting it hang from the broad strap around her neck. "We're finished. I'll let the wedding coordinator know you're ready."

"Thank you for being our photographer," Mia said.

"My pleasure." Lexi winked. She hiked the skirt of her pale pink maxi dress, then hurried across the lawn toward the back door of the church. Her husband, Beau, stood guard over her extra bag of photography equipment. He offered Lexi a bottle of water.

"They're adorable." Eliana gathered Mia's train. "He's so attentive."

"I'm glad they're expecting." Mia smiled as Lexi pushed up on her toes and kissed Beau's cheek.

Lexi had discovered she was pregnant a week before Mia and Gus's wedding. She and Beau still lived in Georgia, near the base where he was stationed. He'd wanted her to cancel her plans to be the wedding photographer, but Lexi had insisted she wouldn't miss Mia and Gus's wedding. She was grateful Lexi hadn't bailed at the last minute, although she felt badly that Beau was so concerned for Lexi's well-being.

"Come on, looks like they're ready for us." Eliana gestured toward the wedding coordinator motioning for them to come inside. Rylee and Tess were standing in the shade outside the church, the skirts of their blue bridesmaids' dresses rippling as they talked and laughed.

Mia picked her way across the grass. The sun warmed her skin. She'd chosen a strapless white gown with a subtle sweetheart neckline and a fitted bodice. Her full skirt, undergirded with layers of tulle, added to the princess effect.

At the entrance to the church, her sisters pulled the doors wide. Inside, her father waited. He looked quite dapper in his gray suit, white shirt and striped tie.

"Your mother and I are so proud of you, Mia." He brushed a tender kiss to her cheek. "It's hard for a dad to give his daughter away, but I am confident that Gus will love you well."

"I love you, Dad." She took the tissue from her bouquet and dabbed at the tears gathering in the corners of her eyes.

She'd reached out to her biological parents, but they hadn't been receptive to her letters. Lexi had confided that they'd stopped speaking to her after she met the Madden family. Mia had hoped they'd change their minds, and the estrangement would end. It was painful to acknowledge that a terrible mistake on a dreadful day thirty-six years ago had shifted the course of their lives.

Thankfully, the people of Hearts Bay and the ones she'd always considered family had continued to love her, expanded their circle to welcome Lexi and her husband. Mia had surrendered her heartache over not knowing her biological parents to the Lord. Because that's all she could do.

The muffled sound of the pianist playing filtered through the double doors. Poppy stood at the front of the line, fidgeting with the ribbon tied on her basket of flower petals. Mia's sisters and her best friend from PA school lined up next.

One by one, they each turned around and whispered words of encouragement, and flashed eager smiles. Her chin wobbled. She prayed she'd hold it together. Blubbering her way through her vows was not how she envisioned standing at the altar.

The wedding coordinator opened the back doors. All eyes shifted their way. Mia's breath hitched as the music swelled. A sweet aroma of roses wafted toward her. She linked her hand in the crook of her father's elbow and squeezed tight.

Poppy led the way down the aisle, her basket of flower petals bobbing in her hand. She grinned at all the awestruck faces lining the packed pews. At three years old she was a handful. It had been a challenge convincing her to wear the white sleeveless dress with the poofy skirt. Mia had promised her extra visits to the ice-cream shop and an endless supply of bubbles and sidewalk chalk.

The music transitioned to her song, and the collective whoosh of fabric rustling as the whole room stood in her honor sent adrenaline pulsing through her veins. With her father beside her, she took the first step toward her future. When the bridesmaids and maid of honor took their places on the left side of the sanctuary, she caught her first glimpse of Gus standing beside the pastor. She couldn't tear her gaze away. He had never looked more handsome. He'd chosen a gray suit that emphasized his tall muscular physique. His bright blue tie only heightened the shades of blue in his gorgeous eyes. She'd run down this aisle if she could.

Instead, with her eyes locked on Gus, she intentionally slowed down.

In the front row, Mia spotted Mom sitting closest to the aisle. She had on a pale blue dress and her dark hair was styled in a simple bun. Her eyes were bright and clear. She didn't need supplemental oxygen or a wheelchair to attend the wedding. At last, her skin was free of bruises. In the past year her health had been restored. Mia would never stop thanking God for the gift of an effective treatment. He'd woven the threads of their stories together to bring her and Gus to this day. Charlie and Abner's deaths had been catalysts for change. Gus had broken free of his hurt and regret. She had been released from her need to be the one who kept order and fixed everybody's problems.

Never had she imagined that the sinking of the *Imogene* would bring Gus back into her life, or that God would grant her the happily ever after she'd secretly wanted but been afraid to hope for. Her long wait for a second chance at love had ended. Today she would become Mrs. Gustav Coleman.

* * * * *

Dear Reader,

People often ask me how I develop ideas for books. Sometimes I overhear a conversation and my imagination takes over. Often a true story featured online or in a magazine grabs my attention. I have wanted to write a story about characters who are switched at birth and I'm grateful that Love Inspired has given me that opportunity.

As always, the creative process has taken me on a journey with the Lord. Writing Gus and Mia's story reminded me of God's grace and redemption, as well as His unconditional love for us. Often we face challenges in our lives that are painful and we worry circumstances won't improve. My hope is that reading this book will inspire you to lean on the Lord's promises and strengthen your relationship with Him.

Thank you for supporting Christian fiction and telling your friends how much you enjoy our books. I'd love to connect with you. You can find me online: https://www.facebook.com/heidimccahan/, http://heidimccahan.com/ or https://www.instagram.com/heidimccahan.author. For news about book releases and sales, sign up for my author newsletter: http://www.subscribepage.com/heidimccahan-newoptin.

Until next time,
Heidi

Get 4 FREE REWARDS!

We'll send you 2 FREE Books plus 2 FREE Mystery Gifts.

FREE Value Over **$20**

Both the **Harlequin® Special Edition** and **Harlequin® Heartwarming™** series feature compelling novels filled with stories of love and strength where the bonds of friendship, family and community unite.

YES! Please send me 2 FREE novels from the Harlequin Special Edition or Harlequin Heartwarming series and my 2 FREE gifts (gifts are worth about $10 retail). After receiving them, if I don't wish to receive any more books, I can return the shipping statement marked "cancel." If I don't cancel, I will receive 6 brand-new Harlequin Special Edition books every month and be billed just $5.49 each in the U.S. or $6.24 each in Canada, a savings of at least 12% off the cover price, or 4 brand-new Harlequin Heartwarming Larger-Print books every month and be billed just $6.24 each in the U.S. or $6.74 each in Canada, a savings of at least 19% off the cover price. It's quite a bargain! Shipping and handling is just 50¢ per book in the U.S. and $1.25 per book in Canada.* I understand that accepting the 2 free books and gifts places me under no obligation to buy anything. I can always return a shipment and cancel at any time by calling the number below. The free books and gifts are mine to keep no matter what I decide.

Choose one: ☐ **Harlequin Special Edition**
(235/335 HDN GRJV)

☐ **Harlequin Heartwarming Larger-Print**
(161/361 HDN GRJV)

Name (please print)

Address   Apt. #

City   State/Province   Zip/Postal Code

Email: Please check this box ☐ if you would like to receive newsletters and promotional emails from Harlequin Enterprises ULC and its affiliates. You can unsubscribe anytime.

Mail to the **Harlequin Reader Service:**
IN U.S.A.: P.O. Box 1341, Buffalo, NY 14240-8531
IN CANADA: P.O. Box 603, Fort Erie, Ontario L2A 5X3

Want to try 2 free books from another series? Call 1-800-873-8635 or visit www.ReaderService.com.

COUNTRY LEGACY COLLECTION

19 FREE BOOKS IN ALL!

EMMETT
Diana Palmer

COURTED BY THE COWBOY

THE RANCHER AND THE BABY
Marie Ferrarella

Cowboys, adventure and romance await you in this
new collection! Enjoy superb reading all year long
with books by bestselling authors like
Diana Palmer, Sasha Summers and Marie Ferrarella!

COMING NEXT MONTH FROM
Love Inspired

PINECRAFT REFUGE
Pinecraft Seasons • by Lenora Worth
Grieving widower Tanner Dawson has no intentions of ever marrying again, but when he meets Eva Miller sparks fly. Giving her a job at his store is the last thing he wants, but he needs the help. As they get closer, can he keep his secrets to protect his daughter?

THE SECRET AMISH ADMIRER
by Virginia Wise
Shy Eliza Zook has secretly been in love with popular Gabriel King since they were children, but he has never noticed her. When a farm injury forces Gabriel to work alongside her in an Amish gift shop, will it be her chance to finally win him over?

REUNITED BY THE BABY
Sunset Ridge • by Brenda Minton
After finding a baby abandoned in the back of his truck, Matthew Rivers enlists the help of RN Parker Smythe, the woman whose love he once rejected. When their feelings start to blossom, could it lead them on a path to something more?

HER ALASKAN RETURN
Serenity Peak • by Belle Calhoune
Back in her hometown in Alaska, single and pregnant Autumn Hines comes face-to-face with first love Judah Campbell when her truck breaks down. Still reeling from tragedy, the widowed fisherman finds hope when he reconnects with Autumn. But can their relationship withstand the secret she's been keeping?

A HOME FOR THE TWINS
by Danielle Thorne
The struggling Azalea Inn is the perfect spot for chef Lindsey Judd to raise her twin boys. But things get complicated when lawyer Donovan Ainsworth comes to stay. Love is the last thing either of them want, but two little matchmakers might feel differently...

HIS TEMPORARY FAMILY
by Julie Brookman
Firefighter Sam Tiernan's life gets turned upside down when a car accident leaves his baby nieces in his care. When his matchmaking grandmother ropes next-door neighbor Fiona Shay into helping him, it might be the push they both need to open their hearts to something more...

LICNM0223